POLISHED OFF

POLISHED OFF

HOLLY JACOBS

The characters and events in these stories are fictitious.
Any similarities to real people, living or dead, is coincidence and not
intended by the author.

Ilex Books 2018
ISBN-13: 978-0-578-18390-9
ISBN-10: 0-578-18390-0

Cover by Kim VanMeter

To my mother, who loved Quincy and came up with this title.
I miss you more than you'll ever know.

CHAPTER ONE

"I'm pregnant."

CHAPTER TWO
TEN MINUTES EARLIER

"**R**ichard Henry Mac Parker, get your hiney off the garage."

It was more than Hank's hiney on the garage … the rest of him was there, too. He was an eight-year-old Houdini, getting in and out of scrapes on a regular basis. When he was with Tiny's nine-year-old son, Caesar, the scrapes were skyscraper in height. "Salvador Addison Mardones, Junior, you too."

"Mom," Hank whined.

"Aunt Q," Caesar echoed.

"Now," I said.

I tried not to notice their route off the garage roof included jumping for a branch in the peach tree, then dropping to the ground.

"Seriously, boys, you are too old for this …" I let the sentence trail off because I was talking to air. The boys were running towards the street end of the driveway where Eli and his wife, LeeAnn, were climbing off their motorcycle.

"Hi, Mom," Eli said as he leaned down and kissed my cheek.

"Hi, kids." I hugged LeeAnn.

After four boys—seriously, four boys—I'd adopted Peri and counted myself lucky as far as daughters go. Then Eli brought home LeeAnn and I was even luckier. She was a dream daughter-in-law and fit perfectly into our weird family.

Probably because she was an actor.

She'd met Eli on the set of *Hands Up Stand Up*. Eli's sitcom based on his stand-up routine. It was a half hour show about a twenty-something cop who moonlights as a comedian. LeeAnn played his groupie slash stalker on the show. Stalker in only the very nicest, funniest, sense.

"Cal's in the house making dinner. Tiny and Sal are coming to pick up Caesar and staying to eat. You know Cal. I'm sure there's more than enough if you want to stay."

"I was going to invite myself regardless," Eli assured me, "And offer to buy pizza. Home cooking sounds even better."

Caesar and Hank were literally climbing on Eli. He grinned, looked at me and LeeAnn and said, "Pardon me a minute," then attacked his little brother and surrogate little brother.

After being the youngest for so long, Eli reveled in being the older brother. He was amazing with the boys.

I frequently asked the boys, *Is that a good idea or a bad idea?*

Most of their ideas fell into the bad idea category.

All of Eli's ideas fell there. Well, except for LeeAnn.

"Boys," I hollered as the whirling dervish of body parts spun on the lawn.

"So what's up?" I asked LeeAnn.

"I can't say. Eli wants to make an announcement." She was grinning, so I knew the announcement wasn't the show had been canceled.

"Are you going to give me a clue?" I asked, just as Cal came out of the house.

It had been almost a decade since we first met and I still could be undone by just his smile.

He shot me one now that made me forget I was pushing fifty.

Half a century.

Seriously. That was so wrong. I didn't feel any older than the girl who'd come to Hollywood with dreams of an acting career. Okay, so maybe I felt a bit wiser than that girl but not older.

But when Cal looked at me like that, I didn't feel like someone who could apply for my AARP card in a few months.

If we weren't surrounded by kids I'd take his hand and lead him right back in the house. We'd forget about dinner and…

"Hi, sweetheart," he said, hugging LeeAnn. "How're things?"

"They have news," I said.

"Good news or bad news?" he asked.

LeeAnn shrugged, but her expression assured him that the news was very good indeed.

"She says we have to wait for Eli to announce it." I turned to the trio on the lawn. Eli currently had Caesar draped over his back and Hank clamped to his legs. "Boys, let Eli go. Eli, what's your news?"

Being the mother of four boys…I knew that beating around the bush never worked, so I went for the direct approach most of the time.

"Mom, we—"

Eli stopped as Tiny and Sal's car pulled in the drive behind his.

They got out of the car and Tiny quickly ran up and hugged LeeAnn, then de-boyed Eli and hugged him..

She started toward me and I knew this could take forever, so I said, "The kids have news."

"Which kids? The big ones or our younger ones? Were you boys climbing on the garage again?" she asked with a mother's instincts.

"Mom—" Caesar whined.

I interrupted his explanation. "Not our two miscreants, though they were on the roof again. Eli and LeeAnn have the news."

"News they need a cop and attorney for?" she asked, looking at my son and daughter-in-law.

"No," Eli said. "I thought I'd tell you all after dinner."

"Eli, you're being mean," LeeAnn scolded. Then she turned to us and said, "I'm pregnant."

There are moments in life that seem to stretch out. Moments where a thousand different thoughts can race through your brain, tumbling one over another in no more time than it takes to blink an eye.

This was one of those times.

My first thought was, *yay. A baby.*

Hank was my change of life baby. I swear, I think I had exactly one viable egg left and he was it. Because it was my last egg, it was a wise egg. Prone to sarcasm and humor that was far too mature for an eight-year-old.

I never admitted that I thought my egg was at fault for my youngest son's snarkiness.

I blamed Eli for Hank's adult sense of humor.

Having a much-older brother who was a standup comedian warped a boy. I couldn't blame the other boys because Hunter was at home in Erie, Pennsylvania. Dr. Hunter. He'd joined my family's medical practice there, which I fondly referred to as the MacPrac.

Miles was working for my ex and he was currently in Vancouver working on a new film. He was gone more than he was here.

So Eli was the boys' biggest influence. He'd warped not only my Hank, but Tiny's Caesar, whose real name was Sal, Jr. And whose middle name was Addison. I'd called him Sal-Ad once and that had morphed into Caesar. And Caesar he remained.

And now Eli was going to have a baby.

And my youngest would only be nine years older than his niece or nephew.

And I'd be a...

Shut the front door...

I was going to be a grandmother.

"It just hit her," Tiny said with all the snarkiness of my youngest. The snarkiness of someone who wasn't almost fifty and realizing she was going to be a grandmother.,

Grandmothers had huge boobs, old lady dresses, and glasses.

I had satisfactory breasts, wore jeans and only needed glasses for reading.

But grandmothers also got to spoil grandkids horribly... then give them back.

I didn't think I'd be very good at giving him or her back.

And that's when all those jumbled thoughts settled into just one... I was in love with this baby I'd only just found out about.

I started to cry.

Later that night, when everyone had gone home and I'd managed to get Hank to bed, I was still in a bit of a grandmother-daze.

So much so that I was thinking about shopping.

I was not a fan of shopping, but suddenly I felt compelled to buy baby stuff.

Images of soft blankets, rubber duckies, and overalls ran through my head.

I did love a baby in overalls.

Cal came up behind me and wrapped his arms around me.

"Penny for your thoughts," he whispered against my neck.

The feel of his breath on my skin was enough to remind me that despite my imminent grandmotherhood and dried up eggs, I was still young enough to feel a surge of lust over this man.

I was pretty sure that even when this baby someday announced that I was going to be a great-grandmother I would still feel this surge for Cal.

I must have been quiet for too long, because he said, "A nickel for your thoughts?"

I took his hand and led him to our room. "I'm thinking that a certain grandmother and grandfather are still young enough to…" I whispered my very ungrandmotherly suggestion in his ear.

He laughed. "That was more than a nickel thought. A lot more."

I laughed as well as I pulled the man I loved and had married into our room.

And I knew without a doubt that no matter how old we got I'd never be too old for this.

CHAPTER THREE

There were a few bonuses to finding out I was going to be a grandmother.

The first being, I discovered that grandmothers were just as attractive as mothers…and the same held true for grandfathers-to-be.

Cal had left a Post-It on the bathroom mirror that said, *I like how you think. Your thoughts are always worth more than a penny to me. I think I owe you more, but this is all I had.* He'd taped a ten-dollar bill next to it.

The second bonus was that I was going to get to spoil that child rotten.

The third bonus was it meant my mother was going to be a great-grandmother.

My son loves me enough that he let me call and break the news to her. I remembered how my mother had reacted to be a grandmother. She'd been thrilled about the baby, but appalled at the thought of grandmotherhood.

I could only imagine how she'd react to the great part.

I put her on speakerphone as I sat in LA traffic on my way to work the next day.

"Quincy, to what do I owe this surprise? It's not Wednesday."

Wednesday was a good day to call Mom. Her office closed early and I could generally catch her on her cell over my lunch break. Everyone at work knew that Wednesdays were my Dr. Judith Quincy Mac days and they steered clear.

Sometimes I wish they'd interrupt with some writing emergency.

The only one who ever interrupted was Dick. If he was around, he'd stop in and I'd put mom on speaker. Those were always good conversations because they loved each other in a totally platonic way. Heck, my dad loved Dick, too.

"I had news that couldn't wait until Wednesday," I said.

"You're pregnant?" she asked.

Honest to pete, my mother was a doctor. You'd think she'd know that by the time you've reached almost fifty your eggs have all dried to dust. I didn't reprimand her, but honestly.

"Better." Frankly, any news was better news than my being pregnant. I couldn't decide if I was flattered or concerned that my mother—a doctor—thought pregnancy was still in the cards for me. "Much better."

"Shoot," she said.

"You're going to be a great-grandmother."

And with that, my mother's side of the line went silent.

Total dead air.

I let her impending great-grandmothership sink in, totally sympathetic about the amount of thoughts that were currently whirling in her mind.

"Which boy?" she finally asked slowly.

"Eli and LeeAnn."

More silence.

"I'm coming for a visit," she announced abruptly. "I'll text you my itinerary."

And that was that.

What had started out as my picking on my mother ended up with me groaning.

I'll confess, I groaned more out of habit than any real problem with my mother's visit. My mother and I were very different people. She'd never really understood me, and if I were fair, I'd never really understood her. She'd been disappointed that I hadn't followed in my family's doctorial footprints. We'd had a rocky relationship, but over the last decade we'd found common ground and had grown closer. So despite the groan, I was happy she was coming for a visit, even if I was bit disappointed my picking on her didn't really work.

Some days the traffic to work riled me up, but today I didn't mind. I turned on music from the Broadway hit, *Dear Evan Hansen*, and sang loudly. Loudly and off-key. But I didn't care. I was thrilled about the baby and happy enough that my mom was coming for a visit.

That happy feeling persisted as I went into work, waving and good morninging my way to the writer's room. "Hi, Lou." "Hi, Freedom." "Hi, Becky and Brenda, Rosanne…"

HeartMark had built us a new studio…okay, it wasn't just for us, though we were the only show that had used it to date. They'd given us a huge stage. It was big enough to house all three of our Cereal moms' kitchen sets. And we had a connected stage for swing sets.

I'd never done a single camera sitcom slash murder series before, but enough of the crew had commented about how lucky we were, that I counted my blessings. Frequently a show's writers' room is removed from the action. They're lucky if they're next door to the stage, but ours was upstairs with other offices.

I loved walking through Beth, Maggie, and Joanne's kitchens. They were at the center of the show.

Beth, with her sweet hominess was reflected in the antiques and older décor…classic white appliances, stoneware jugs as decorations.

Maggie with her efficient no-nonsense style shone through in the sleek modern design of her stainless steel and grey kitchen.

And our central mother, Joanne's Bohemian spirit radiated from her funky kitchen with her neon green stove that sat next to a Hoosier cabinet.

I could have gone the back way, but frankly, I was feeling nostalgic and spent more than a few minutes admiring all three kitchens. We had two more episodes of *Cereal Killers*. Dick and I wrote the last scene two years ago because we knew we wanted a true and honest ending.

We knew exactly where it would happen—all three moms at Joanne's, sitting around her purple table, drinking coffee. We'd even written the dialogue, their fast-paced, talking over one another, coffee swigging dialogue that the show had become known for.

One reviewer had mentioned that we'd made coffee a central character to the show. I hefted my travel mug to my lips and took a sip of my coffee, certain that my own personal ambrosia deserved to be heavily showcased.

Cal once wondered aloud if I loved coffee more than him. I'd promised him I loved him more…at least most days.

I smiled at the memory as I continued to look around.

Part of me was sad to put the show to bed. I'd loved working with Dick on *Cereal Killers*. We'd been talking to the network about a string of *Cereal Killers* movies. We were the HeartMark Channels number one show and they had offered us another season, but Dick and I agreed it was best to go out on top.

Reoccurring movies was a nice way of keeping the show alive without the weekly grind.

And we were working on a new idea.

By working, I mean we kept tossing out ideas to one another, then literally tossing them out. We wanted to do something that was the same...but very different. We hadn't hit on the right idea yet.

Dick kept assuring me we would, but I couldn't help but feel that maybe we'd run our course.

Maybe *Cereal Killers* was our last hurrah.

It was a less than cheery thought that blunted my happy mood just a bit.

I took the last sip of coffee from my mug as I climbed the stairs to the offices and writers' room. That made me smile. Whenever I could make my to-go coffee make it all the way to the office, it was a good day. I threw my bag down on the long table in the writer's room, annoyed that there was no coffee aroma filling the room. Syd, our intern, had obviously not made the coffee yet.

I walked around the long table, my eye on the prize— the lovely coffeemaker on the corner of the snack table— and suddenly found myself flat on the floor.

It hadn't been a very hard landing because something had broken my fall.

I propped myself up slowly and found myself staring at the face of a zombie.

A dead zombie.

Yes, zombies by their very nature are dead, but I could immediately see this wasn't a normal dead zombie.

This was a dead-dead zombie.

This was a zombie that someone killed.

How did I know that this zombie had been murdered?

For one thing, rigor mortis had set in and there was a small hole in his forehead with evidence that blood had bubbled at the edge of the wound. There wasn't much though. No, not much at all because the rest of the blood had flowed out of the back of his head where I assumed there was a large, gaping hole.

It pooled on the floor, making a blood puddle around his head.

Having worked on *Cereal Killers* for so long, I knew a thing or two about dead bodies and bullet wounds. Much more than I knew when I'd found my first dead body.

Once again, time warped and things flitted through my head in the blink of an eye.

I realized that this was the third dead body I'd found.

I had worried after the first two that I was going to become the Hollywood version of Jessica Fletcher and spend the rest of my life stumbling over dead bodies. The decade between body number two and this one had lulled me into a false sense of complacency. I'd almost forgotten about my JF (*Jessica Fletcher*) fears.

I noticed that the hole looked like a .380 or that Saturday Night Special gun that we used in the first season. A sort of small hole where the bullet entered, a larger one in the back where it exited. A smaller caliber would have left the entry hole, but the bullet probably wouldn't have exited. It would have simply bounced around in his skull.

We'd done enough scenes on the show for me to be pretty sure I was right. Freedom Carter, our make-up artist was an expert and I'd seen wounds like this…only when the scene was done, the victim went home.

Today's dead-dead zombie wasn't going home again.

All these thoughts were still tumbling about my head as I saw I was on a dead body and sprang up.

Yes, sprang.

I might be closing in on fifty and an almost grand-mother, but when I fell on a corpse I could rebound with a youthful spring.

While some people might simply scream when they found themselves on a dead body, after the first two I had a bit more decorum.

"Three?" I screamed.

Yes, after three bodies, I could scream real English words after my discovery.

Dick and I had done an interview with Stephen Colbert after *Cereal Killers* won its first Emmy. I knew he'd ask me about the two dead bodies I'd found.

I'd been compared to Jessica Fletcher before and looked up her stats. Two hundred and seventy-four murders in a town of Cabot Cover, Maine, which had a population of only three thousand five hundred. Stephan and I had joked that it was amazing that Jessica Fletcher had ever been allowed out of her house. It was a bigger miracle that the local police hadn't wondered about someone finding almost ten percent of the town dead.

Los Angeles has a population of almost four million and I felt a spurt of fear over the fact I'd just found my third dead body.

Thoughts of my favorite uncle and tattoos floated through my thoughts as I hurried out of the room.

From vast personal experience I knew I didn't want to touch—much less clean—anything.

I hurried to the door just as it started to open. Thank goodness it was Dick. "We've got a dead body," I screamed. "Another freakin' dead body, Dick."

Before I could add, *call the cops*, he said, "I know. What I don't know is how Ajax is going to get rid of it before Beth and the kids come home."

"No, not a writing dead body. Not some fictional dead body. Not a *Cereal Killers'* dead body. There's a dead zombie on the floor."

Dick had the audacity to chuckle. "Aren't zombies always dead by definition, Quincy?"

Jokes?

He was making dead zombie jokes?

Okay, it was hard to be too annoyed, since I'd had the same thought myself.

"Those guys are always wandering over here," Dick continued, moving toward the floor and noticing the splatter of something I missed as I entered and would have to guess was brains on the wall. Then he noticed the body in the pooling puddle of blood on the floor.

"You found another one?" he asked weakly.

"I know. Three. Who finds three dead bodies in one lifetime?"

"Angela Lansbury on a regular basis. But Jessica Fletcher was fictional. I think if you're real and keep falling over dead bodies you might find yourself not getting invited to many parties."

I wondered if Stephen Colbert was interested in doing a jailhouse interview with me. I shook my head, feeling oddly calm. "I don't like Hollywood parties, but still it's nice to be asked."

I pulled my phone out of my back pocket and rather than call 911, I called Cal.

"Hey, honey, how's it going?" he asked. "Did you like my note this morning?"

It seemed like a lifetime since I found that ten dollar bill taped to the mirror.

"Hank cleared out the rest of my cash, but your thoughts are always worth a lot more than a penny to me. Speaking of Hank, I dropped him and Caesar off at school on time and I'm just heading into a meeting with the mayor."

The *on time* part was because last week he got the boys there late and Hank had been livid. He might be a terror who can't stay off perfectly good garage roofs, but he was a punctual terror.

As if he could sense this wasn't a normal phone call, he stopped talking and asked, "What? What happened?"

"I was hoping you could send someone over to the studio quietly," I said. "I don't want it out over the radio. Maybe Charlie?"

I could almost hear him freeze.

"Are you okay?"

The fact that his first concern was my safety warmed me, which was enough to let me realize just how cold I'd been.

Shock.

I was probably in shock.

"Yes. I'm okay. I fell and—"

"Quincy, how bad is it? I swear… Listen, don't call the cops, call an ambulance. I'll meet you—"

"No," I said, forcefully. "Listen, I'm fine. You see, fell over a dead zombie. A dead-dead zombie."

"Quince, don't kid me like that," he said, sounding less upset.

I knew I had to be clear and explain what had happened. "I'm not kidding. There's a dead zombie in the writer's room. I found him when I tripped on him."

"Over him?" Cal asked.

"No, *on* him." I did a little cootie shake. I'd found two other bodies, but this was the first one I'd landed on.

Cal chuckled. "Honey, I know it's not your genre, but zombies are by their very nature, dead. One of your extras working next door coming back for a visit?"

"Dick made the same joke, but Cal, this isn't a joke. Whoever the actor is playing that zombie is dead in a decidedly human, not zombie, way. Like I said, he's a dead-dead zombie. I found a third dead body," I said as an aside. Three. "And I don't know if I know him, since he's in zombie makeup. It could be someone who worked here in the past."

That would explain why there was a dead zombie in my writers' room. I tried to imagine what he looked like without the makeup, but didn't think I knew him.

"A third one?" Cal repeated weakly.

"Yes. I don't think I know this one, but it's hard to tell with the zombie makeup and the hole in his head. Just send someone quick."

"I will," Cal said. "It can't be Charlie—he's family—but we'll send someone. We'll send his best guy. You're sure you're okay?"

"Yeah. Dick's with me."

"Both of you stand outside the room and shut the door," he said, all cop and all business. "Don't let anyone else in."

"Okay. I knew that. I'm better at this protecting a crime scene than any non-cop should be."

He sighed quite audibly over the phone. "And Quince?"

"Yeah?"

"I love you."

"Love you, too," I said, feeling steadier.

I called the studio security and then put the phone back in my pocket and looked at Dick.

"Look at it this way, the show's going to get a lot of free press," Dick said.

I must have looked horrified.

He shrugged. "It's Hollywood, Quince. There's no such thing as bad press."

"Unless you're the one who keeps finding dead bodies and ends up in jail," I said.

"You're not going to jail."

"Remember Stephen Colbert? He agreed Jessica Fletcher should have been investigated as a serial killer."

"Oh, yeah. Colbert. I bet he wants to book us again after this. And maybe, when we've wrapped up *Cereal Killers*, we could use this as a spin-off. We could—"

I interrupted my friend. "I don't want to talk about potential new murder mystery shows. We need to get out of this real life one first. The older boys will weather this murder okay, but what about Hank? He's so young. You're right, this is going to get press." I groaned.

And despite Dick's proclamation that there was no such thing as bad press, I had to ask, "Dick, what about the show?" I immediately felt horrible that there was a dead body in the writers' room and I was worried about the show. "We'll have to close it down."

"Not necessarily. It depends on who's dead."

"Dick—" I said with shocked admonishment, though I suspected there was a kernel of truth to the statement. This was Hollywood and the show must go on ... unless the zombie was some network big shot.

I didn't get to finish because Lou, one of our security guys came around the corner.

"What's going on?" he asked. "I just got a call and—"

"There's a dead zombie in the writers' room," I said.

"It's probably just someone from next door sleeping it off." He reached for the door handle as if he were going to go in and check.

I stepped in front of him, blocking his entrance. "I'm sure he's not normal zombie dead. He's a dead-dead zombie. His brains," I shuddered at the memory, "are on the wall. And you can't go in."

"I'm security," he said and puffed up his chest.

"Yes. And the cops are coming. They're on their way and left instructions no one is allowed in the room."

"But I'm security," Lou said again.

"Yes. But you're not a detective."

He gave me a look every woman recognizes. It was a look that said having a woman defy him more than annoyed him. It pissed him off.

He took a step closer. For a moment, I thought he was going to push me aside, but then the sound of more people turning the corner and coming towards us apparently made him rethink that plan. He took a step back.

"Quincy, what happened?" Soho Morning (honest to pete, that was her name), this episode's director, asked.

I realized that Soho had only directed a couple of Cereal Killers episodes. Could she be the killer?

How about Lou? He was certainly angry at the moment. I didn't feel like he was going to kill me, but hey, if we were alone in the writers' room late at night and he was this angry?

"There's been a murder," I said, watching both Soho and Lou's expression as what I said registered.

Soho didn't say anything as she digested my statement. As understanding dawned, she looked shocked and said, "Not again."

Lou didn't look the least bit shocked. "That's a premature conclusion," he said all huffily, but not in the least bit guiltily.

I glared at him. "No, not really. The zombie's brains are on the wall and there's a non-zombie hole in his head."

Lou was annoying me.

And being annoyed was better than being afraid.

"Let me go steer everyone clear of here," Soho said helpfully. "Should I have them stick around?"

"Yes. I'm sure the detective will want to get names and at least some preliminary statements," Dick said. "At least that's how Quincy and I would write it."

Soho nodded and took off downstairs.

"I think I should go check for a pulse," Lou said again, taking that step forward again, just as Detective Charlie came up the stairs.

"Quincy, what the he—"

"Heck," I filled in. "Charlie, I don't know what to tell you. I tripped over a zombie and it's clear he's dead. Lou, our security guard, was trying to go in but I wouldn't let him. I was the only one inside and I know tripping over the zombie ruined evidence. I'd finished my to-go coffee and was going to coffeemaker for a second cup and that's what I was looking at then... there he was. Or rather there I was on top of him."

And it hit me all over again. I'd fallen on top of a dead body.

It wasn't just the thought that hit me, it was the realization that I'd been on top of a dead body.

I felt my knees start to buckle, and felt Dick holding my arm, steadying me.

"Quince, are you all right?" Charlie asked.

Charlie and I hadn't gotten off to a great start, but we'd become friends over the years. More than that, we were family.

I nodded. "Now that you're here, do you mind if I go sit down? I'll be down the hall in my office when you're ready to talk to me. I know the procedure by now."

Alas, I knew it all to well.

"Sure," Charlie said looking concerned. "I'm not going to investigate this because we're friends and I'm not in the field anymore, but I have one of my best guys coming in. I'll just wait here until he arrives then find you." He looked at Dick. "Why don't you get her something to drink?"

Dick led me down the hall.

I muttered, "Unless it's whiskey, don't bother."

"Is Cal coming?" Dick asked, choosing not to fight with me.

He and Cal had become good friends as well. But this wasn't a matter of friendship, but rather him thinking Cal might make me behave.

Might was the operative word.

I nodded, acquiescing to his unasked request. I wouldn't drink until after Charlie's new detective interviewed me. Then all bets were off.

Whenever you fall on a dead body, you probably deserved to get as drunk as you wanted to get.

We sat in my office, a room I didn't use nearly as often as the writers' room.

My mind was scattered. Realizing that since the body was in my writers' room, there was a chance it was someone I knew. Soho, Lou were only the tip of the iceberg. Cast and crew. Security guards. Directors. We had a rotating group of regular directors, and occasionally tried out someone new-to-us. Any of them would be familiar with our set up.

Who.

What.

Where.

Why.

Someone I knew. A stranger.

And then there was the question who was dead? When you were wearing zombie makeup, it could be hard to know what you really looked like, but as I stared at his zombified face, there was no sense of familiarity.

How were we going to shoot the last two episodes?

How about everyone who worked here? Would the new detective grill everyone? The front gate had records of everyone who came in and out. That might narrow the field. But still, it was a big studio and even at that it was a big pool of suspects.

And what if someone snuck on? It wouldn't be that difficult. And if you were hiding in someone's trunk, like Ajax hid in Beth's car. She hadn't even known he was there.

From zombies, to *Cereal Killers*, to witnesses, to suspects…whirl, whirl, whirl. I was drowning in my own thoughts.

I tried to stop the spinning thoughts and pin one down. I finally managed to realize people would be coming in to work. "Oh, we need to tell the cast and crew who're not already here not to come in. Maybe leave word at the gate …"

"I'm on it," Dick said as he pulled his phone out of his pocket.

I looked down and realized there was something red on my shirt. Was it make-up blood or real blood?

Finding my first dead body had been a shock, especially when I realized that I'd cleaned the murder weapon. The second dead body had been just as shocking, though I was blood-free on that one.

This time I'd landed face-first in it.

On it.

On him.

Literally, I'd faced death.

I wanted to take my shirt off and shower for an hour, but I knew better.

I waited for Cal or Charlie to come find me.

And as I had the thought, there he was—Cal strode into the room and reached out as if to hug me, but I stopped him. "I'm covered in … er evidence. I think I should wait for the new guy to get here. I've got some clothes in my closet to change into."

"Are you okay?" he asked as he searched my face, looking for the answer.

"I think I did everything right this time. I didn't clean anything." I tried to shoot him a smile, but I didn't think I'd managed it. "Once I realized that the zombie was dead and not just zombie-dead, I called you and secured the room."

"That's perfect, Quince," he said softly.

I shook my head, which was better than allowing my entire body to shake as it felt like it wanted to do. "I fell on the body. I'm sure I left DNA all over it, especially since I obviously have his DNA on me. Unless it's zombie blood. God, I hope its fake zombie blood, not real blood."

I wanted to claw at my bloodied shirt, but didn't. "Do you think the new detective will be here soon? I wish Charlie were investigating. He would know it wasn't me."

"I'm sure the detective is checking out the room. And I'm sure he doesn't think you did it. And Quince, it could be natural causes."

I shook my head. "There were brains on the wall and a bullet hole in his head. I'm pretty sure that's not natural."

I shuddered. I was feeling worse and worse with every passing minute.

"Do you think we can keep my name out of the paper? I mean, the older boys are used to it, but poor Hank. Do you think I need to call Sal to represent me?"

"I don't think so," Cal said. "Just tell the detective the truth."

"You know how I feel about jail and tattoos." I'd Googled where tattoos change the least with age. My options were my inner forearm, neck, back, and upper part of my chest. So many things sag with age. Over the years I'd decided that the only thing worse than a tattoo was a saggy tattoo.

"I think you're fine," Cal said.

But he was wrong. I wasn't fine. I'd been feeling worse and worse and I finally gave up, dashed into the bathroom and threw up.

Shortly thereafter, Charlie's great detective came in. He looked like he was twelve and said his name was Detective Duncan Daugherty. He was tall and thin ... the mom in me wanted to feed him something.

He asked me what happened, took notes, and allowed me to change out of my stained clothes and into something clean. He put my zombie gooed clothes in a paper bag and took them away with him after he said he'd be in touch.

"Do you think that's it?" I asked Cal who was leading me to the car.

He sighed. "Probably not."

"Should I stay? I'm sure they'll be talking to whatever cast and crew are here. Maybe they need my support and—"

"I talked to Dick and he's staying put. He didn't have the shock of falling on the body. He'll handle things. You know you can count on him." Cal kept talking. I'm not sure about half of what he said. I stared out the window, but I couldn't tell you what way he drove home.

Somewhere on a highway I remembered something.

My mother had called to say her flight was due to land at five o'clock

It was too late to call and tell her to cancel the trip.

Things could not get worse.

CHAPTER FOUR

Things didn't get worse. They got better. I decided then and there that I needed to get back to approaching life from a more optimistic outlook. Although, tripping over a zombie—a dead-dead zombie—might make anyone's optimistic nature wobble.

Mom called as we walked in the house. She'd made it as far as Detroit, then caught a flight back home because she was asked to pinch-hit for a conference whose keynote speaker was in the hospital.

There's an irony to a doctor speaking at a medical conference calling in sick.

When I mentioned that, my mother said my humor was warped, but then chuckled and said he was going to be fine and she was tickled to be speaking.

She warned me this was just a temporary hiccup. She was coming to LA soon.

I was happy for the reprieve. I didn't tell her about finding a third body. I told myself it was because I didn't want to worry her or ruin her speaking engagement, but truth was I didn't want to talk about it.

"I'm going to take a shower," I told Cal.

Normally, he'd offer to take one with me or if Hank were around waggle his eyebrows to let me know he was thinking about showering with me.

Normally, I'd say yes, or at least feel appreciated with the eye-waggle.

Today was not normal. He did neither. He simply said, "I'll go start some tea."

Tea made me think about my friend Cathy who worked on *Dead Man Walking*, the neighboring zombie show. I wondered if she and her husband Steve knew yet? I wondered if they knew the zombie? I felt sick that this was going to hurt them.

I nodded at Cal and hurried into the bathroom and took a shower until the hot water gave out.

I put on my oldest sweats and an old police t-shirt of Cal's, then padded barefoot into the kitchen.

He handed me a mug of tea and reminded me that, "Tiny's picking up Hank."

"We're going to have to tell him," I said. "And I need to tell the other boys and Tiny and—"

"We'll tell them, Quince. I'll make any calls you want."

I reached across the counter and took his hand.

This man.

From the moment I saw him, I knew that he was my perfect fit.

He'd argue that I didn't know. That I'd been afraid he was going to arrest me for a murder I'd cleaned up. He'd say that I hadn't trusted him.

Maybe on the surface, but I think my heart knew the moment I saw him that he was my one.

It just took the rest of me a while to catch up.

We heard the car pull in the drive. I got up and walked to the front door.

I felt nervous as Hank got out and ran to the house, looking excited. He'd probably aced a test and I was going to ruin his excitement by breaking the news.

He burst in the house and said, "You found a zombie? A real live zombie in your office. Cool."

He knew?

Tiny and Caesar came in after him.

"Are you okay?" she asked.

I nodded, then asked my youngest, "How do you know?"

"Mom, it's all over the internet. All the guys were texting me. Their parents read about your zombie and it's so cool."

Tiny nodded. "My phone's been ringing off the hook. Theresa said the office has been flooded with calls from clients trying to get some dirt."

I sighed.

"Do you need Sal?" she asked.

I shook my head. "Not yet at least."

"Are you going to jail, Mom?" Hank asked, still not sounding upset. If anything the idea of me going to jail sounded as cool to him as me tripping over a zombie.

"Dad wouldn't let her go to jail," Caesar said with a son's pride in his father.

"Yeah, well, she fell on a zombie," Hank said, as if suddenly that wasn't quite cool enough.

In a city where so many people worked in television and film, my job wasn't anything out of the norm. But falling on a zombie? I guess even in a town where weirdness was normal, that was over the top.

"It's sad, buddy," I said. "Someone lost their life."

For a moment he looked sober, but a blink of an eye later, he asked, "Do you know who he was?"

"No. I—"

"Hank," Cal said firmly, interrupting me. "This was a horrible situation. Your mother's distraught. It's not cool at all."

Hank nodded slowly and tried again to look more serious, but I could see he was still impressed. "Are you going to solve this crime, too?"

I shook my head. "No, sweetie. I'm going to leave it to the police."

Cal looked at me and nodded his approval.

Tiny looked skeptical. When the boys raced back to Hank's room for something, she said, "Come on, Quincy. A zombie?"

"I'm sure it was someone from the show next door," I said. "This murder has nothing to do with me."

"None of them had anything to do with you until they did." It was almost a joke, but she was too concerned for me to pull it off.

"Are you okay?"

"Yeah. It was a shock, but I'm fine."

"You'd better call your mom and kids. The internet is spreading this like wildfire. By the time the news is on, it'll be all over."

The Internet. Back when I was young, no one would have heard anything about my zombie discovery until the news that night or even the next morning.

But now it was everywhere in seconds.

It turned out, I didn't need to make any calls. The phone started ringing off the hook and binging little notices that I had text messages. I didn't pick up unknown or blocked numbers, but I did pick up friends.

All my sons called.

My mother got wind of it. "I should have said no to the talk. You need me."

"I'm fine, Mom. Charlie put his best detective on the case." I didn't mention the boy looked about twelve. "By the time you get out here, he'll have it all figured out."

My brothers and sisters-in-laws called.

Peri called from Texas.

Honey called.

Lottie called from home in Erie, Pennsylvania.

Theresa called. She'd called in sick all those years ago and I'd filled in for her the day I'd discovered my first dead body. Maybe if she hadn't been sick, she'd have found the body and...

I realized if that happened, I wouldn't have met Cal, had Hank, met Dick, or started my career in television and movies...a career I loved.

I was glad that Theresa had called in sick all those years ago. And if not for my inadvertent amateur sleuthing, I wouldn't have met Rob, Theresa's husband, and neither would she.

I realized that even when horrible things had happened in my life, they'd moved me someplace I was happy to be. Maybe there was a lesson in accepting life as it came—the good and the bad.

Eventually, I'd talked to everyone I needed to and had my answers down pat.

I was sure the zombie came from the show next door.

It had nothing to do with me.

I wasn't going to try to solve this murder on my own.

I wasn't worried about jail or tattoos.

I woke up that night with nightmares about zombies haunting me, but I didn't need to be a shrink to realize that was normal. When you fall on your face and find you've landed on a very dead zombie, nightmares are a given.

I was having coffee the next morning when Dick called, saying we'd been given the go-ahead to get back into our studio. The writers' room was still off limits, but we could film the last two episodes of *Cereal Killers*.

That's the thing about Hollywood…it really does embrace the motto, *the show must go on.*

Soho directed the second to the last show and Sean Mulcahy was our director for our very last episode. Sean had directed my movies for HeartMark and the entire cast and crew loved it when he could find time to shoot an episode. We thought this would put our final week of work on a high note.

And we all tried.

But the yellow tape across the writers' room door cast a pall on the festivities.

Real life didn't work like my show. *Cereal Killers'* unanswered question about who killed Tricia Booker and why were all answered in the last two episodes. In real life, we hadn't got any answers about the zombie.

In the show, the cops caught the killers with the help of our amateur sleuths' assistance. My three moms ended the last episode at a kitchen table, sipping coffee as they had every episode.

Everyone who should, got their happily-ever-after.

Everyone who shouldn't went to jail, presumably for a very, very long time.

It was too bad it wasn't like that in real life.

No, in real life, the coroner said the dead zombie's name was Brad Michna. He was an extra on *Dead Man Walking,* the apocalyptic zombie show that filmed next door.

His name didn't ring a bell for anyone. And when they showed us his picture, we weren't any more helpful.

And though there was a dark cloud over the last days of filming the show, it was almost back to normal…well, as normal as the end of a show can ever be.

We had a huge final cast party at Le Celebre Hotel after we put the finale episode to bed. My friend, Honey

Martin was a chef at their restaurant, Psst, and she did a beautiful job. Her husband, Big G. was beaming over her success.

There were a lot of speeches. I made one and so did Dick.

"Thank you all for making the show such a joy to work on," I said.

"I hope we're all back together again soon working on a *Cereal Killers* movie," said Dick.

We'd heard that given the show's sudden notoriety, they might hurry a Cereal Killer movie into production.

I wasn't sure how I felt about that. On one hand, the thought that I'd get to work with people I really like again was wonderful.

But there was a kind of slimy second feeling that we were capitalizing on a man's murder that tainted the first one.

I pushed the second feeling aside as I worked the room.

Sean came, along with his wife, Dee.

Our cast and crew were all there.

We partied the night away.

At the end of the night, after I'd talked to pretty much every person at the party, I found myself in Cal's arms in the middle of the dance floor.

This man.

It was a thought that I'd had a regular basis.

He leaned down, his breath tickled my ear as he softly said, "The luckiest day of my life was the day you cleaned a murder scene and I met you."

My knees went all wobbly.

After all our years together, Cal was still my favorite person ever.

My other favorite moment of the night was as we left, Dick called out, "See you Monday. I have an idea."

HeartMark was interested in a new show from us, and we planned to spend the next few months fleshing something out.

I almost forgot about visions of tattoos.

Things were looking better.

CHAPTER FIVE

The following Tuesday, my rollercoaster ups and downs continued.

Things were looking even worse than worse.

Not only was my mother's flight early in the morning but I had to listen to her go on and on about how no one in the rest of my doctor family had ever discovered a dead body. I reminded her that they'd all declared people dead from time to time, but she assured me that wasn't the same thing.

We'd found common ground, my mother and I, but sometimes we slipped back into old patterns. This was one of those times.

"Mom, it's not like I intended to trip over and *land on* a dead body." Even after a couple weeks, I still got the heebie-jeebies thinking about landing on a zombie.

Brad Michna, I corrected myself.

The zombie had a name.

And as far as anyone could tell, there was no connection between Michna and *Cereal Killers*... or me. I guess if you were going to land on a dead body, it was best if you had no motive for making him dead.

"I'm sorry, honey," Mom said. "I worry. And sometimes my worrying doesn't come out that way."

I reached across the car and took her hand. "Thanks, Mom."

"I love you, Quincy."

And just that easily, we were back to our common ground. "I love you, too, Mom."

We got back to the house before Hank had to go to school. Having breakfast with Cal and Hank seemed to further calm her down.

I tried to think about how I would feel if Miles, Hunter, Eli or Hank found a dead body and felt a bit more sympathetic towards my mom and her concern.

"Grandma, wanna take me to school today?" Hank asked. "It's show-and-tell and the teacher said you could be my show."

My mom kissed his forehead. "I would be honored to be your show." As he scampered from the room, she asked, "May I use a car?"

"Sure," I said. I'd have a bit of respite and that was worth being carless for the morning. "Dick's coming over later. I'll have him pick us up some lunch on the way."

"From Honey or Big G?" she asked.

"Definitely from Honey or Big G." Having friends who were chefs at restaurants meant I ate very well.

"I'll see you at lunch then," she said.

My morning suddenly seemed brighter. I started to think about our new idea for a young, single mother who opens her own PI firm called *Skye Jones, Private Eye.* I wasn't overly enamored with it. We needed a better hook. A better character.

Something like …

That's when the phone rang. I answered reflectively. "Hello?"

"Hi, Quincy, it's Detective Daugherty."

Baby cop was calling. I had a feeling it wasn't good news.

No, if it was good news, he'd have said something like, *I've got great news* with a lilt in his voice. Yes, that's how you started a good news conversation.

But on the off chance I was wrong, I said, "Did you catch the murderer?"

That would definitely be good news.

"No. I've got a question," he said.

"Shoot." I realized that was unfortunate choice of words for someone who'd recently found a zombie who'd been shot.

I changed it to, "Go ahead."

I had a sinking feeling in the pit of my stomach, though a simple question in and of itself wasn't ominous.

"Have you ever seen *Behind the Scenes?*"

My sinking feeling sunk a bit lower. "I don't listen to it, but yes I know about the podcast. They did a podcast on our show a few years ago. *LA's newest writer should go back to cleaning toilets, because this series is a bunch of...*"

I realized who was asking and knew the question had to do with my zombie. Maybe *Behind the Scenes* had done a podcast on Brad Michna... that had led to a true hit job. If that was the case, baby detective wasn't asking to hear me complain about the podcast's negative comments about my show. I had a sinking feeling as I asked, "You asked about *Behind the Scenes* because?"

"The host only uses his first name... Brad. But his last name is Michna. Our zombie Brad Michna was the show's host and..."

My dead zombie had been very negative about me and my show. In law enforcement circles that is known as *Motive* with a very large, capital **M**.

Baby cop went on to talk about getting a warrant for info on a VPN, then on the server and...

It was all Greek to me.

"Does this mean what I think it means?" I asked weakly.

"We're going to have to come back and talk to everyone from *Cereal Killers* since he was killed on your set and someone there might have had a problem with him."

By someone, he meant me.

Visions of tattoos once again floated through my head.

I'd get all my kids' names and Cal's, I decided. In Harry Potter characters had tattooed *dark marks*. I'd have heart marks... to remind me of those I loved as I suffered through my dark prison years.

I liked the idea of heart marks. Maybe I'd mention that to someone at HeartMark... it would make a killer ad campaign.

Killer reminded me of why I needed my own *heart marks*.

I sighed and said, "Yeah, that's what I thought it meant."

Duncan wanted to come talk to me later this afternoon. I said yes. I'd have started to call the cast and crew, but he'd asked me not to. He wanted to spring the information on them and see their reaction.

I felt a bit better that he'd told me on the phone and didn't seem particularly concerned about watching my reaction.

I said I wouldn't mention it to anyone—I was confident that no one in my cast or crew had done it—then hung up.

So I did what any maid, turned writer and occasional amateur sleuth would do... I went down to the basement and got out my white-board and was setting it up in the dining room when my mother got home from being Hank's show-and-tell. Dick pulled in right after her, two take-out bags in hand. They came in together.

"Hey, Quince..." he started, then saw my expression. "What happened."

36

"Brad Michna was driving force behind the *Behind the Scenes* podcasts. He was the *Brad* that hosted it and investigated the stories." I saw that Dick immediately understood the implication.

Mom did not. "What is behind the scenes?" she asked.

"A podcast," Dick answered. "With a host who creeps around Hollywood shows, looking for dirt. He did a hit piece on Quincy a couple years ago. He said, 'This maid in LA is all played out,' and reviewed *Cereal Killers*, saying it was sophomoric and—"

"And it would be easy to believe I carried a grudge," I filled in.

My mother who only a few hours ago had railed against my finding a third dead body, squared her shoulders and said, "So what are we going to do about it?"

"We?" I asked.

"We," she said firmly. "No daughter of mine is going to jail and getting a tattoo."

My father and brothers were doctors. My brothers' wives were doctors. I had been an aspiring actress, maid, business owner, and now I was a writer. For a long time I thought my doctor mother was disappointed in me. Turned out she simply didn't understand me. But she loved me.

I hugged her. I felt her surprise and then she hugged me back. "I love you, Quincy. Mac's don't do tattoos."

"Uncle Bill has one," I pointed out to tease her.

"You know that wasn't his fault," Mom said. Uncle Bill was the true black sheep of the Mac family. Even if he'd gone to jail for a crime he didn't commit, he had a tattoo. And Macs didn't have tattoos. I was pretty sure I was too old to get one, so we needed to solve this murder.

"Let's get started," I said. "First step, let's find out about this podcast."

"I'll start watching episodes of it," Mom volunteered.

"Listening," I corrected.

She nodded.

"I'll make some calls and find out more about Michna's shows," Dick said.

"And I'll call Rob and see what he can tell me about the *Behind the Scenes* site," I said.

Rob Williams had helped me before. He was a computer nerd extraordinaire. He was married to Mac'Cleaner's worst maid ever, Theresa. She wasn't a good maid, but she was a fantastic manager and ran our original Mac'Cleaner store, which thrived under her control.

Rob and Theresa had a zillion kids. Okay, so just four right now. But if you were at their house, it was easy to believe they had a zillion. It was very, very loud.

Their kids were so loud they made Caesar and Hank seem quiet.

I walked into the living room and dialed Rob.

"Quincy, I heard you'd found another dead body," he said by way of salutation. "This is how people get reputations."

"This is how people go to jail," I said more grumpily than I meant to. "Any dead body after your second dead body makes you fair game as a suspect. Only I didn't do it."

I explained who the dead body was and my connection.

Rob let out a long whistle and said, "Okay, so let me do some digging and I'll call you back."

"Don't do anything illegal," I warned. "Theresa would kill me if you went to jail and she was left all alone with the kids."

Rob laughed. "She'd never forgive either of us for that fate worse than death. I'll be careful."

Before Cal got home, I'd heard back from Rob and we'd put together a good start. There was Brad Michna. He was unmarried, one kid showed up on his Facebook page, but only pictures from when his son was younger, so it didn't look like they were close ... or maybe his kid simply didn't want to be part of his dad's Facebook feed.

As far as anyone could tell, Michna had no significant other. He'd made the rounds of shows, playing an extra in crowd scenes here and an occasional dead body there. He'd been working as an extra on our neighbor, *Dead Man Walking*, when he was killed. He'd played a zombie in a zombie mob scene.

I might write a comedic murder series, but I didn't understand zombie shows, despite the fact they were all the rage for the last few years.

I guess I was a simple woman. Give me one dead body and a murder to solve rather than a hoard of dead bodies that walked, moaned and ate brains.

Rob said he hadn't found anything unusual about Michna's podcast. He'd used a VPN, a virtual private network. It was all gobbly goop to me, but Rob said he'd keep digging.

Cal came home, took one look at the white-board and said, "What happened?"

"I am not going to jail or getting a tattoo," I said as I left Mom and Dick to work and pulled Cal into our room.

I told him about Duncan's call.

I waited for him to laugh and assure me that I was safe.

"I know that Duncan called me, and I take that to mean he didn't feel the need to see my reaction, but Cal, the fact he did one of his podcasts on me and the show—that's motive. The fact I'd practically forgotten the incident, doesn't matter. The fact that I haven't ever listened to Michna's podcasts, doesn't matter. I might not be a detective, but I write them and I know that his piece on me gives me motive with a capital **M**."

Cal nodded. "It does. I can take a leave from work and work this with you on my own time and—"

I shook my head. "It means the world to me that you want to do that, but Cal, if anything happens to me, I don't want you involved. We have Hank to think of. You have your career to think of. You and Charlie said Duncan is one of your best detectives. Let's trust him to get to the bottom of things."

Cal nodded toward the room I'd just left. "But you don't trust him."

"I do. I'm just adding a layer of insurance. He doesn't work in the business. I do. Something that might not mean anything to him, might mean something to me and Dick. And if I find anything, I'll tell Duncan right away." I crossed my heart. "Promise."

Cal pulled me into his arms and hugged me. It wasn't sexual. It was meant to be comforting. And yet, I felt that old familiar spark as I snuggled closer. "I love you," I whispered.

"I love you, too. And I'd give up anything, including my job to keep you safe."

"I know that. But things have changed with Hank. I swear, we'll leave the investigation to Duncan. We're just doing some looking to see if there's something he might not realize. If things go south, then we'll reassess."

He nodded. "I'll stay out of the dining room."

"Thanks for trusting me."

"More than that, Quincy, I love you."

I felt more than a sizzle of awareness as we walked out to rejoin the others. I felt warm and mushy.

I took his hand in mine.

This man.

I don't know how I got so lucky, but this man was worth everything I'd gone through in the past.

And he was worth everything I'd be fighting for now.

The next day, I joined Mom listening to Michna's podcasts. Every podcast was basically a hit piece and added more names to our suspect pool. We kept that growing list of people on the whiteboard.

But even his worst shows didn't seems that crazy bad by Hollywood standards. Who was sleeping with who. Who cheated on who. Who was making more money on a show than the rest of the cast. There were a few times he got his hands on upcoming scripts and leaked them.

I mulled that over. Dick and I would be annoyed, to be sure, if someone leaked one of our scripts. Even outraged that someone had leaked it, but not outraged enough to kill someone.

When I heard Hank come in, I left the dining room and closed the door.

We'd talked about renovating the house and making it more open-concept, but I'd never really felt the need and I was glad now that we'd left it with dedicated rooms … and doors.

"Mom, did you find the murderer yet?" Hank asked as he ran in.

"Honey, I told you I was going to leave it to Uncle Charlie's detective. Detective Duncan seems like a nice guy."

Hank snorted. "Nice doesn't mean good. And he's not as good as you and Uncle Dick."

I didn't point out that Cal might be hurt that his name wasn't on Hank's list, but I let it slide. "If I didn't think Detective Duncan could handle the case, I'd ask Dad to step in."

"Yeah, Dad's good, but you're better. I mean, he's had cases he couldn't solve. You solved all yours."

I kissed his head to hide my smile. He had a point, but one that I wouldn't be sharing with Cal. "I think your dad's had a lot more cases, so—"

I was talking to myself. Hank was pulling on my arm, obviously ready to share something else. "Mom, me and Caesar talked. We're gonna help. We can go undercover. I mean, who'd suspect two kids of investigating a murder? Maybe you and Uncle Dick should think about that for your next show? No one thinks of kids as investigators."

Now there was logic in his statement, but I wasn't about to admit that. And I wasn't going to point out my childhood favorite series, Trixie Belden, was a kid detective. Maybe if Dick and I couldn't come up with a new show idea we could think about making an updated Trixie Belden show?

I shook my head and got myself back on point. "Detective Duncan has it handled, Hank. But thank you for the offer."

He nodded, but had that look in his eyes I recognized because I'd seen it whenever he promised not to climb on the garage roof anymore. It said, *I'll just say yes and then do as I please.*

"Young man, you will not have anything to do with this."

Cal had freaked out when I'd tried to help with investigations. I couldn't imagine how he'd react to Hank and Caesar trying to help.

"Now, how about your homework?" I said just as the door opened and Cal walked in.

"How was everyone's day?" he asked. He looked around and said, "Where's your mom?"

"She's out with Eli and LeeAnn. She said something about shopping."

Cal kissed my cheek and mock-shuddered. "I've seen your mom shop for the boys. Imagine how she's going to be with her first great-grandchild?"

"The advantage is, she'll take the pressure off me having to shop." Normally I hated to shop, but I'll confess, shopping for the grandbaby did have some appeal. Soft blankets, Onesies, toys...

I looked at Hank. "Homework," I said.

"But Mom," he whined as he stomped towards the kitchen where I was sure he'd find a snack before he started. Lucky for me, his three older brothers had taught me a lot about where to hide the Poptarts. All he'd find were the apples and carrot sticks.

"Any news?" I asked Cal as soon as Hank was out of earshot.

"Quince, you know even if there was, I couldn't share information on an active investigation with you. You asked me to keep this on the up and up, remember? Plus, I gave the case to Charlie's squad just because it wouldn't be ethical for me to be involved because I'm helplessly in love with the prime suspect."

He laughed as he said the words and I knew he was joking.

Yeah, I knew it, but it didn't help my sudden nervous stomach that kicked in as visions of tattoos floated through my head.

Cal must have seen my panic. "Honey, I was just kidding. You know you're not the prime suspect."

"But I am *a* suspect," I said. "I've got Motive with a capital M, remember?"

"Everyone on both sets could technically be considered a suspect. But I vouched for you. You were with me the night of the murder."

"But you just said you loved me. So that baby detective might decide you loved me enough to lie for me. Dick and I have never found spouses or lovers to be the most reliable of alibis in the show."

"Honey, there's a difference between real life and television. You're going to make yourself crazy."

"I've been listening to Michna's podcasts. If that's the suspect pool, I'm still on the list. And I have another strike against me because I fell on the body. If I were writing that scene, I'd say it was a smart way for a murderer to explain any DNA on a victim. And my only alibi is you."

I was sunk.

Cal kissed me again. "I swear, if you go to jail, I'll bring you a cake with a file in it."

"You don't know how to bake a cake," I grumbled.

"Big G does and he'd help. So would Honey."

While he was right, I couldn't shake the feeling that the cops weren't going to solve this one.

I tried to ignore the feeling as I helped Hank with his homework, got dinner, and oohed and aahed over Mom and LeeAnn's shopping trip finds. Mom insisted on getting the *MamaRoo* out of the box and setting it up to show me. It would rock the baby in many rhythms, including backseat of a car.

"It is amazing," LeeAnn murmured as she watched the seat swing rhythmically. She had a far away look in her eyes that said she was picturing her baby in the seat. And suddenly, I could almost see it. My first grandchild. I could imagine holding him or her. Snuggling him or her. That new baby scent.

My heart constricted.

"Oh, your poor father," Mom said. "He'd have given anything to have something like this. You had colic. Car rides were the only things that soothed you. We never had a problem in the world with your brothers, but you marched to your own beat from the get-go. Your dad and I were both working and ..."

I let my mom prattle on about my colic and I suddenly remembered new babies weren't all snuggles and new baby scent. New babies were puke, poop, and partying at three a.m. New babies were colic, constipation, and nipple confusion.

I smiled as I realized that even the downsides of a new baby didn't dim my excitement. I fell back into watching the space-age baby chair and picturing my grandchild. I had to confess, the picture was pretty amazing. And I couldn't fault my mother her awe or even her complaints over my colic. Miles had colic as well and it was a trial.

"Mom," I said, hoping to slow her down.

"Yes?"

"I'm going to the studio tomorrow morning. Would you take Hank to school?"

She gave me that mom-narrow-eyed look that said she was suspicious about my motives for going back. "Sure honey," she said slowly.

"I feel bad for leaving you. Even though the show's shut down, I have a few things to clear out." I crossed my fingers as I said the words. They weren't precisely a lie, but they weren't precisely the truth either.

Macs by their nature didn't prevaricate. But as always, I was the family black sheep. And I *was* going to clear the last of my stuff from my office.

Then I was going to head over to *Dead Man Walking* and talk to the writers for the show. Steve and Cathy were good friends.

Maybe they'd have some suggestions on who on their set would have wanted to kill Brad Michna.

"Thanks, Mom," I said and turned back to the new baby talk.

CHAPTER SIX

Steve Cade had white hair. Not grey. Not salt and pepper…white. When he smiled, I'd have sworn in a court of law that his eyes twinkled. If he grew a beard and wore some padding, he could play Santa anywhere. I knew it wasn't really that he looked like Santa, but his hair reminded me of that jolly old elf. And whenever he spoke with his clipped British accent, my Santa fantasy gave way to a dapper, Father Christmas one.

Of course, Steve made his living dealing with zombies, guts and gore. That was pretty anti-Santa.

Suddenly, I wondered if he'd chosen this show because he wanted to be an anti-Santa?

"Quincy, love, how are you?" Concern etched his face as he swept me into a friendly hug.

"I'm okay. How's our lovely Cathy? I thought I'd see her here." Cathy and Steve not only worked together on the show, but genuinely seemed to enjoy each other's company. You rarely saw one without the other.

"Cathy's knackered and I made her take the day off—"

A tiny woman with blondish brown hair opened the door and said, "Steve, honestly, Craig's late and I don't know how I'll have him ready in time—" She spotted me and stopped. "Sorry, I didn't know you had a meeting."

46

She turned her head and I saw a big green streak in her hair. It was a fun look. If I weren't about to be a grandmother I might think about adding a streak of color to mine.

"Ann, Quincy's the one that found Michna," he said. "I imagine that's why she came over, though we hadn't got that far yet." He shot me a Santa-twinkle.

"I'll take care of Craig," she said. "I just wanted to give you the heads up." She shot me a funny, sympathetic looks and shut the door.

Steve picked up where he left off without skipping a beat. I knew that in this business, interruptions were par for the course. "Cathy's been so upset. The entire *Dead Man Walking* cast is a mess over this. We're close. A family really. But you know how that is. So this has us all rattled. I can't think of anything that would interest Michna about us. I can't imagine anything that would make us fodder for his show. Do you think he was working here to find some story on one of us?"

"I don't have a clue. And I can't imagine what he was doing in our writers' room."

"Maybe he was doing a story on someone at *Cereal Killers*. He did a podcast about you before, didn't he?" Steve asked.

I sighed as I nodded. "Yes. But saying he wasn't enamored with our show shouldn't be enough of a reason for anyone to murder him. For any of *us* to kill him. We have our ardent fans, but he wasn't the first one to complain that we've made a murder mystery, warm, cozy, and funny."

I never understood that complaint, but some people liked dark and brooding … *Cereal Killers* was never that.

Steve gave me a wry smile. "Some people just don't have a sense of humor about murder. They get their panties in a twist over."

I thought about tripping over Michna and shuddered. I was glad that the show was over, because I suddenly didn't find murder nearly as funny either.

Murder was all fun and games until you were the one facing jail time for a murder you didn't commit.

"So you can't think of any reason he'd be targeting your show?" I asked.

Steve frowned. "None. Can you?"

"No," I admitted morosely.

"Well, I guess we'll just have to leave it to the police then." He studied me a minute. "You are leaving it to the police, aren't you, Quincy my love?"

"Of course," I lied. "I'm married to a cop. I know what fine work they do. I trust that they'll get to the bottom of things."

Steve nodded, looking satisfied. "Well, then. Have you and Dick got a new show to pitch? I hear the studio would really like a follow up to *Cereal Killers.*"

I nodded. "We've been tossing ideas around. Nothing concrete yet."

"I hope to have you back next door next season."

I stood. "That would be nice."

"And don't forget my offer. Anytime you want to play a zombie extra, you've got it."

"It'd give me nightmares," I said with a laugh. "But Hank would think I was the coolest mom ever. And I'll confess, I always have fun *Stan Lee-ing* things in my movies." When we made my first movie, Steamed, based on that first dead body I'd discovered, I'd insisted I get a Stan Lee cameo. I didn't pop up in every episode of *Cereal Killers,* but if you watched the show carefully, you could find me as an extra in more than a few episodes.

Even Dick had got in on the game.

Being on *Dead Man Walking* wouldn't be quite the same, but being cool to Hank might be worth it.

Steve had made the offer before. He cracked himself up at one party, talking about me wearing a zombified Halloween maid's outfit. "Think about it. It would be so much fun," he said.

Steve was sweet and looked like Santa, but he was no help.

I went back to my office, gathered my last boxes and left.

I was out of work.

I was a suspect—although I felt I was only nominally one—of another murder.

I glanced at my watch. I had to pick up Hank in half an hour.

I hurried toward the school and played another of Michna's *Behind the Scenes* podcasts. It was from a month ago.

"I followed Janet Mann to the bar and figured, bingo, here we go. It's Hollywood and there's only one reason a star from *MissChief* would be heading into a dingy dive like The Bit Part Bar."

The bar name made me freeze. It was the bar Willy owned. As in Willy, the murderer of Mr. Banning...my first dead body.

It had a new owner, but that was about all that had changed about it. It was still a dive.

"No luck," Michna said in the podcast. "She met her husband, if you can believe that. And she put some country music on the jukebox and line-danced with him. Yeah, that's not much of a scandal. But as I sat there, drinking a beer, watching Janet and her husband dance, I noticed someone in the back booth next to me. Someone I recognized. She's not a big Hollywood name, but she is associated with a show you all know. I'm going to do some digging. I think there might be a story here—"

Someone thumping on my closed car window made me jump. I turned off the podcast and hit the button to unroll the window, though I already wished the line was moving so I would have an excuse to get out of here.

"Adrienne, how are you?"

The tall, blonde ran most of Hank's school singlehand-edly. I desperately tried to think about what was next on the calendar.

"Are you coming to the Halloween Party tomorrow afternoon?

Lie. Lie. Lie, I told myself. But telling didn't quite reach my lips because I found myself saying, "Sure."

"Great. We had some parent helpers back out and you can fill in for someone. See me at ten when you get here. Toodles."

Before I could ask what job she wanted me to do, or tell her I couldn't be there at ten, she was gone.

"Toodles?" I muttered.

Who said toodles?

"Hey, Mom. Guess what?" Hank said breathlessly as he got in the car. Without waiting for my guess, he continued on at a breathless pace, "Me and Caesar got picked to be in the band tomorrow. Well, not really in the band. We're gonna be making the shaker noise for the one song. I can't tell you which one, 'cause we're not supposed to tell. It's a surprise. But they had our class go to some rehearsals and me and Caesar got picked. And Britta and Liz, too. But they're girls."

"Hey, I'm a girl," I protested as we made our way out into traffic.

"Nah, you're a mom. That don't count. But anyway, you can watch for me, right?"

"I wouldn't miss it," I promised.

For someone who was currently out of work, I felt as if I were busier than ever. I had a business meeting next week with Tiny. I was no longer an active part of Mac'Cleaners, but I stayed informed.

Dick and I were still working on a new pitch for the studio.

Mom was here for another few days.

I was volunteering at the Halloween party.

And I wanted to find out who killed a dead zombie in my office.

"Mom. Hey, mom?" Hank said.

"Sorry honey. What?"

"Can Caesar sleep over tonight? We want to make our own costumes for tomorrow."

"Do you need help?" I asked.

"Nah, we got a great idea."

"Sure he can. Call Aunt Tiny and see if he's allowed."

I glanced in the rearview mirror at my surprise baby. I liked that term better than change-of-life baby, which made me sound ancient. He grinned and said, "Great. Thanks Mom."

And with all those other things I had to do, I had to remember that I had a eight-year-old who desperately needed me. So tomorrow, I'd forget all the other things I had to do and concentrate on Hank.

I'd forget all about zombies.

The next morning, Cal, Mom, and I were in the kitchen drinking our after-lunch pot of coffee as we listened to Caesar and Hank laughing and occasionally shouting upstairs.

They'd both asked for old clothes they could destroy.

The thing about eight and nine year old boys is they had more old clothes than good clothes.

We'd all asked if they needed help, but they swore they were fine.

"Boys, we need to leave," I called up the stairs.

"Coming, Mom," Hank called down.

The boys thudded loudly as they walked down the hall. Then thudded even louder as they walked down the stairs.

They'd dressed as … zombies.

Ugh.

For two kids, their makeup was excellent.

I put on a fake smile and said, "Wow, guys. Those are great."

Hank's darkened lips grinned. "Freedom taught us."

Freedom Carter was our makeup artist.

"She said she does more dead bodies than zombies, but she figured it out," Hank said.

I'd planned on forgetting zombies today, but it looked like that wasn't going to happen. I simply smiled and said, "You guys look great."

Cal shot me a look over Hank's head saying, *what are you going to do.*

I smiled and shrugged, which meant, *there's nothing to do but roll with it.*

After all these years, Cal and I didn't need words. We could speak without using any. It was a bit of magic in my opinion.

"You guys have fun at the Halloween party," he said. "I've got to go in for a few hours."

I nodded as I kissed him goodbye.

"He's one of the good ones," Mom whispered as we headed out to the car.

Mom and I might not agree on everything, but we did agree on this. "Yes he is."

Hank and Caesar dragged my mom towards the fun when we got in the gym, and I found Adrienne. The Halloween party was always so much fun. There was a ton of good volunteering options. I hoped I got the donut-on-a-string booth.

I didn't.

I got kitchen duty.

When I went to the kitchen, Ruthy Mantis, who ran one of the coffee stalls at the studio, smiled and said, "Quincy, we all know that murder and mayhem is more your thing than cooking."

Rats. She remembered my cupcakes last bake sale day.

In my defense, not being allowed dairy, sugar, or wheat products really does put a damper on baking options. But I'd tried. I'd used oatmeal, applesauce and lots of honey.

They were a bit flat, but I thought they were edible.

The kids did not.

I will point out, that a few of those wheatless baked goods tasted a bit wheaty to me, and I had my suspicions that there might have been some sugar in a few.

Ruthy smiled. "We found you a job you can't mess up."

I was on garbage duty.

I really don't think there are many worse jobs at a grade school than picking up garbage. I did find that mine weren't the only inedible healthy snacks ever.

I picked up a practically uneaten plate of gluten free donuts when someone called out, "Hey, Quince."

I turned around and grinned when I spotted Julie Iron, one of *Cereal Killers* costumer designers.

"Hey, Julie. How're things?"

"I'm home all day with four kids. I need to get back to work asap. I actually cleaned out the closet yesterday. I found clothes I wore in college in the back. They're back in style again. I told my husband that that's why I never throw anything out." She laughed. "How about you?"

"Dick and I are still working on the new idea."

"Any hints?" she asked.

I shook my head and pretended to lock my lips.

"I saw the boys. Did Freedom help them?" she asked.

"Yes. They kept it a secret from me and it really threw me for a loop when they came down."

Julie laughed. "Any news on your dead zombie?"

"Not my dead zombie," I corrected. "Nothing more than what's been in the paper. He's part of *Behind the Scenes.* I think that just increased the suspect list exponentially. Michna hit most of the major shows in town."

"Didn't he do one on the show?" she asked. "It was before I came to the show."

I nodded. "It didn't hurt our ratings at all. I'd forgotten about it until I heard who he was."

"Well, you must be nervous about the fact you have motive and the zombie was found in our writers' room. Your writers' room."

I wanted to say, *What the heck, Julie?*

If I weren't already nervous, I would have been now.

I knew she didn't mean anything by it, but my smile felt as fake as the smile I'd used in my short-lived toothpaste campaign back in the day.

I said, "I trust the cops to get to the bottom of it." I picked up the plate of uneaten donuts and tossed them in the garbage.

Julie must have sensed that she'd struck a nerve. "I'm sure you're right," she said. "I better go see what the kids are up to."

"Catch you later," I called after her rapid retreat.

Despite my hope of forgetting about Michna today, he was very much on my mind.

And obviously he was on everyone else's.

Julie was just the first in a long stream of people pumping me for information about Brad Michna, Hollywood's new favorite dead-dead zombie.

It might take forever to drive from point A to point B in LA, but it truly was a small town. Everyone knew everyone. And everyone wanted to know everyone else's business.

It just so happened my business contained more dead bodies than the rest of the world's.

I gave the same responses over and over as I picked up trash.

No, I didn't have any other information.

Yes, it was shocking.

No, I wasn't investigating. I trusted the police to get to the bottom of it.

Yes, it was a horrible way to end our series.

No, I wasn't planning to include zombies in my next show.

Speaking of zombies, Cathy Walker practically ran me over. She was a tall, sweet woman who always had a smile and always seemed to be laughing.

A tiny woman who looked vaguely familiar followed her.

"I missed you the other day," I said.

"I was deathly sick and it's taking me forever to recover," she said. "I saw the doctor and he's put me on a new vitamin regime. There's been a horrible bug going through the cast for weeks, but…" She shrugged. "Oh, I'm so rude. Quincy, do you know my friend Ann? She was down with the bug for a couple weeks. Ann Abner DeMarco, this is Quincy Mac."

"Nice to meet you," I said, trying to figure out where I knew her from.

"Oh, you're the one who—" Ann stopped short.

I nodded. "Yeah, I'm the one."

Ann turned her head and I noticed a small purple streak and realized I'd seen her at the studio at least once. Her hair had been green then, I was pretty sure.

Cathy looked sympathetic. "Steve said he talked to you, but I wanted to add my own I'm-so-sorry-this-happened-to-you," she said the last words in such a rush that they sounded like one long word. "It has to be someone who thought they could capitalize on your past. I hope this doesn't mean you're going to be the dumping ground for future dead bodies."

She laughed.

From some people it might have sounded like some kind of dig, but Cathy wasn't that kind of person. I found myself laughing with her. Ann just stood there looking awkward.

Maybe when you worked with zombies or serial killers (cereal killers?) every day you get a warped perspective.

Then Cathy sobered up. "I think whoever left the body with you did it thinking it would throw the investigation off. But they didn't really think it through. Killing poor Michna there guaranteed you'd look into it. You've never not-solved a case, Quincy. I'm sure you'll figure this one out."

Her words echoed Hank's the other day when he assured me I was better investigator than his father because I'd never not solved a case.

Cathy patted my shoulder. "If you need a break or a shoulder, you just head over to the set. There's always a cup of tea and a friend there." She smiled and said, "Now, to blatantly change the subject, I hear Steve was trying to zombie-fy you in your maid's outfit."

"Maid?" Ann asked.

"Quincy owned a cleaning business and was working as a maid when she found her first dead body?"

"First?" Ann chirped right on cue.

"Ann Arbor DeMarco is newish to Hollywood. She's only been here a few months," Cathy said.

"A year now," Ann corrected.

"First dead body?" she repeated.

I'll confess, it was rather nice to have someone not know the story. For years, it seemed everyone did, but most had seemingly forgotten, but remembered if prompted. Ann's blank look was nice.

"First," I said. "Hopefully the current zombie dead body is the last one."

Ann looked as if she wanted to say something more, but Cathy just kept talking.

"Back to Steve's lovely idea," Cathy said. "You should definitely say yes. It's a scene that would be memorable and…"

"Lovely?" I supplied, smiling.

Cathy laughed on cue. "That's just it."

I had noticed that both Cathy and Steve used the word *lovely* a lot. I had Joanne on *Cereal Killers* pepper her dialogue with the word. It was my own personal homage to Steve and Cathy.

Ann looked between us, as if not sure what the joke was. Before I could fill her in, the principal announced the concert was going to start, I found myself agreeing to talk to Steve about my potential zombification.

"That's lovely." I shot her another look and she laughed as she continued, "He'll be chuffed, I'm sure. Come on, Ann dear, let's find the minions."

"It was nice meeting you," Ann called as she hustled after Cathy.

I thankfully left my cleanup duties behind and moved to the front of the gym to the small stage.

Four of the grade school's older kids had formed a band called *I'll be as Famous as Them*. IBAT. I knew the kids all had parents who were in diverse bands... country, rap, and pop. They were really good for thirteen year olds.

I didn't recognize the song with its refrain about *Which, which one*. I suspect it was in the band's playlist because of the repeated word *which... witch*. I got it.

My heart about burst when I spotted the boys. They were in the back row, shaking their maracas with gusto.

Which one?

Which one?

Which one?

The band sang, the boys shook, and I beamed.

I got lost in one of those mom-moments.

You know, those moments when your heart grows all Grinch-like and turns to a giant ball of mush all at once.

My other boys had long since stopped needing me. Oh, they needed me in some ways, but not in that all encompassing way they had when they were little. They were grown and leading their own lives.

I don't think I ever truly enjoyed moments like this back then. After my ex, Jerome, tossed me over for a new model, I was overwhelmed with working, supporting the kids and meeting their needs. There wasn't time for standing back and enjoying them.

At that moment, Cal was suddenly next to me. He put his arm over my shoulder as the boys sang.

You.

You.

You.

"You," he whispered in my ear.

I had everything, I realized.

I had a career I adored, Cal standing beside me enjoying the moment with me and a family I adored. I felt overwhelmed with gratitude. Gratitude that I was old enough to recognize how amazing these moments were.

Cal glanced at me at that moment and smiled, before he looked back at Hank. My heart got even mushier.

The first time I met him there'd been a rush of awareness.

Of course, he was investigating a murder and I was the prime suspect.

He'd deny it if I brought it up, but seriously, I cleaned the murder weapon. How could I not have been a suspect?

My attempts to "help" with the investigation had annoyed him.

Somewhere along the line, annoyance gave way to something else entirely and here we were, a happy, old married couple who were about to become grandparents.

I felt that warm rush that I felt every time I thought about being a grandmother.

Cal looked again and there was a question in his eyes. I leaned toward him and whispered, "I was just thinking how lucky I am."

"How lucky we are," he corrected then pulled me close, his arm still resting on my shoulders as we watched the rest of Hank's performance.

We clapped loudly—embarrassingly loudly—after they finished.

We started walking toward the stage and for a moment I lost Cal in the press of parents.

Someone pushed into me, almost knocking me down.

I turned around and no one was there.

I didn't give it another thought as I made the rounds, visiting with parents I knew, helping out with the kids' games.

It was a good day.

No murder or mayhem.

Not a dead body in sight.

It wasn't until I got home that night that I realized murder and mayhem didn't take a day off.

I took off my jeans and emptied the pockets. A couple bobby pins, a hair twisty, and a note folded up like a football. It looked like something that Lottie and I might have passed back in our school days.

I thought about her and the star-shaped glasses she'd given me all those years ago when I left for Hollywood. I made a mental note to call her soon.

Speaking of notes, I figured I must have picked up someone else's note somewhere along the day. Probably when I was on garbage detail. Then I saw a Q. on the paper.

I opened it.

It read:

> *This is not a MAID for TV movie.*
> *Stay out of it.*

This?

It didn't take a cryptologist to decipher this note.

Someone didn't want me looking into this murder.

I was pretty sure *Maid* wasn't a typo. They were referring to my being a maid who cleaned a murder scene...then turned the experience into a movie.

Someone slipped the note into my pocket at the Halloween party.

It had to be when I got shoved after the concert.

I tried to picture who had been standing around me.

I couldn't come up with a single name. I'd only had eyes for Hank, Caesar, and Cal. Always Cal.

Speak of the devil.

Cal came into the bedroom, pulled off his shirt and dropped it on the floor. I thought about showing him the note, then thought about covering up the note by making a snarky comment about *I might be a maid, but I'm not your maid… pick up the shirt.* But seeing him without his shirt on froze those words in my throat. I shoved the note back in my pocket, then let the jeans fall to the floor.

I'd talk to Cal about it later. Right now, I had other things on my mind.

"Come to bed," I said.

"I was hoping you'd ask," he said with that sexy smile that always turned my insides to mush.

For a long, long time, I didn't give the note another thought.

Next morning, I not only gave the note a thought… I couldn't stop thinking about it. I knew I should tell Cal.

But I was afraid if I did, he'd make me stop looking into Michna's murder.

I wasn't ready to do that. I'd obviously caught someone's attention.

I also didn't say anything to Mom as I tucked her back on a plane headed to Erie, Pennsylvania that morning.

"Now, if you or Dick find anything, you call me. I wish I could stay. I keep threatening to retire. Trips like this make me seriously think it might be time. I could spend more time with you and the kids. And I could fill in for your dad and the rest at the practice when someone needed time off or got sick. That way I'd still be working, I just wouldn't be working as much."

She looked more serious than I would have anticipated.

"Really? You'd retire?" I'd never even considered the possibility. Mom was a doctor, through and through. I'm not sure what she'd do without work.

But she didn't look as if she had as many doubts as I did. She nodded. "Your dad and I have been talking about it. There's more to life than work."

I shook my head and half joking, half serious asked, "Who are you and what have you done with my mother?"

She laughed. "We're taking a pottery class starting next week."

"Who we?" I asked, expecting her to admonish me for poor grammar.

She didn't. She just laughed and said, "Your father and I…we."

Thinking of my mother and father sitting in front of a glob of clay at a wheel was disturbing. It didn't fit with my ideas of who my parents were.

My parents, my brothers, and their spouses were all very busy, serious people. The shared a medical practice and a sense of purpose.

I had never given any thought to my parents retiring someday.

I'd never pictured them not working at the Mac-Prac, my personal term for the Mac family practice.

"What would you do all day?" I asked.

"I might be a pottery prodigy. Maybe I'll make pots and mugs all day. Or maybe I'll take up belly dancing."

"Belly dancing?" I asked weakly.

She nodded. "I read an article that said it's great exercise. And your dad and I could take all kinds of classes. We've been going to the Jefferson Education Society lectures more often. Erie's full of things to do. And we want to travel and spend time out here with you. We've talked about buying a condo so we could visit without becoming a burden."

"Mom, you're not a—"

She interrupted me with a laugh. "Quincy, if I came and spent a month, I'd be a burden. Guests go bad after a few days, just like bananas."

"You're bananas," I teased, but we both knew she was right.

She kissed my cheek. "We haven't decided, but next time I come to town, we're going to take a look around. I'd like something with a water view. Close to you, but not too close."

I looked at my mother. Though our relationship had changed for the better in recent years, I still always saw her as my-mom-the-doctor. Suddenly I saw, my-mom-the-person, and it was a good look on her.

"I'd like that, Mom. I mean, I'd really like that. Come back soon. We'll go look."

She kissed my cheek. "Keep me posted."

"I will."

"And Quincy, don't do anything dangerous. I don't think I could stand it if you got hurt. I love you."

First my mom was thinking about retiring, now she was worried about me and saying she loved me? I didn't quite know what to do with that, so I simply said, "I love you, too. Come back soon. Bring Dad."

"I will. I've got this first great grandbaby on the way. Even if we hadn't talked about retiring and spending more time here before, we'd be talking now."

I dropped my mom at the airport and then headed to Pattycake's Pancake House to meet Dick.

Since all the evidence seemed to lead back to someone at the studio, I didn't want to meet there. And I didn't want to take a chance of Cal overhearing us, so I didn't want to meet at home. And Dick's house ... well, imagine ninety year old hermit meets bookworm and you'd have a feel for his sense of design. There were bookshelves and books every-where. I like books as much as the next guy (or gal), but it could be a bit claustrophobic.

He was sitting at our table and waved as I made my way back.

"Quincy, they have a porter pancake," he said with a lot of enthusiasm.

"Porter?" I had no clue what a porter pancake was.

"Beer."

Dick seemed inordinately excited about beer pancakes. I wasn't quite so sure, I decided to stick to the regular but-termilk variety and steal a bite of his to test it out.

Orders placed, coffees in hand he said, "I was mulling over our next pitch. It's lackluster and I think we both know it. That's why we've stalled, but then I had an idea. *Mass Murder.*"

I knew he was talking about a title, but teased him. "I suspect that's not a good thing to say in a public venue."

He laughed. "Picture this…an old Catholic priest under suspicion for a series of murders. All the victims were his parishioners. It doesn't look good. The bishop puts him on leave—"

"I don't know if that's what the church calls it," I said.

He shrugged. "We can figure that out. You know what I mean. Anyway, he's on the outs and no one believes him, except one old nun. Sister Mary Faith."

"I think nuns are named after saints."

Dick shrugged again. "There must have been a saint named Faith. That's beside the point and you know it."

I did know it. When you were writing fiction, whether it's a book or a script, you can fill in those kind of technical details. The point is to have a good idea to build the piece around. A solid base. Nothing we'd come up with yet felt solid enough to support a series.

Dick went on, excitement oozing from every word. "The nun and a young novitiate work together and investigate the murders to save the priest. Maybe he's in the hospital, so he can't do it himself. Oh, that's good. Maybe he's sick and everyone knows it, so the real murderer tried to pin the murders on the priest, thinking he'd go to the grave and everyone would think the murders were solved."

I should have been thinking about murders and priests, but my mind was on the note and the overriding sense of guilt that I hadn't told Cal.

"Q.?" Dick said. "You don't like the idea?"

"No, I do like it. It seems a little dark like this, but what if the murderer was some sort of vigilante whose victims were predators from the intercity neighborhood? I mean, they're still a murderer and that's wrong, but the victims are reprehensible."

He nodded so enthusiastically he reminded me of Hank. "Oh, that's great. An innocent novitiate and a world weary older nun?"

"Switch it," I said. "The novitiate came with baggage. The older nun lived in a cloister until she felt called into the world and into the city, but she's naïve."

"Yes." Dick started scribbling on his ever-present notepad. After a few minutes he looked up and said, "What's wrong?"

I shared Dick's excitement for this idea. I had that feeling in the pit of my stomach that said this was a winner. We could make this into something. But right next to that feeling was one of guilt. It crept around the edges of my excitement, weighing them down. "I am a horrible person and an awful wife."

Our pancakes arrived, but Dick left his porter pancake untouched. "What did you do?"

I reached in my pocket and slid the note to him. "I didn't show it to Cal."

Dick read it, then looked at me. "You were afraid he'd say stay out of it because it just got too serious."

I nodded.

"Quincy, I've never known you to bow to pressure from anyone. When you feel you have to do something, you do it. But I also don't think you're the kind of person who lies to her husband."

"I didn't lie," I said. The statement about not lying felt like a lie.

"A lie of omission is still a lie," he said quietly, voicing my thoughts like any good writing partner would.

I nodded.

"So you know what you have to do," he said. "Eat your pancakes, then go find Cal and the detective."

I sighed. "I hate it when you're right."

But that was a lie, too. I was grateful because Dick was saying what I already knew. I had to tell Cal.

Dick laughed. "I'm right so often that it must be a dreadful burden."

I felt better, knowing what I had to do. I dug into my pancakes as Dick took a bite of his. "Oh, this is great. Wanna bite?"

I took him up on his invitation and took a bite.

Porter pancakes don't taste very beery. They tasted pancakey. And Pancakes at Pattycake's were always good.

He nodded. "Now, about the priest. What dread disease does he have?"

We chatted about priests, nuns, and murder as I ate my pancakes. Then, knowing I wouldn't feel right until I came clean with Cal, I stood up. "I better go face the firing squad. Can we meet later to do some more work? This really is a great idea."

Dick nodded. "Text me when you get home."

Feeling a bit like Marie Antoinette heading toward the guillotine, I left the restaurant and drove to the station.

I went to Cal's office, hoping he'd be somewhere else doing something else, but I wasn't that lucky. He smiled as he saw me come in. "What brings you here? Did you and Dick come up with something?"

"I think we did. But that's not why I'm here."

He frowned. "What did you do?"

"Something happened and I should have told you last night, but I didn't. I felt guilty and realized I needed to tell you and so here I am. You should probably call in Duncan, too."

"Quincy, I…" Cal stopped and shook his head. "Okay. You're here now. Tell me."

I pulled the note out of my pocket. "Someone slipped it into my pocket right after the concert on Saturday. I know I should have told you then, but I knew you'd say I needed to stop and—"

Cal interrupted me. There was an angry edge to his voice—or maybe it was disappointment—as he said, "You don't have a clue what I might have said because you didn't give me the opportunity to."

"I'm sorry," I said. Even if he was angry with me, I felt so much better for having told him. "I mean, really sorry. I should have shown you immediately."

He got up, walked around the desk and kissed me.

That was not the reaction I anticipated. "What's that for? Not that I'm complaining," I added hastily.

"Because we have definitely made progress. For a moment you reverted to your old investigative practices, but then you remembered I am not your enemy. I am always, always on your side. No exceptions. Always."

I stepped into his embrace and for a moment remembered exactly why I fell in love with Cal. I might frustrate him, annoy him and even make him angry, but he loved me. Completely and truly.

That kind of unconditional love is a true gift. I felt humbled and overwhelmed.

"I love you," I said, my voice muffled against his chest.

"Of course you do. I'm amazing. How could you not?"

I started laughing as I tightened my embrace.

At that moment, Detective Duncan came him. "Sorry, I can come back."

We broke apart and Cal said, "No. It's fine. I was just reminding Quincy of how lucky she is to have me. And also reminding her that she needs to come to us the minute she finds anything."

"Anything? Like?" Baby detective gave me an intense look.

Cal took the note and handed it to him. "This. Someone put this in her pocket at the school's Halloween party yesterday."

Duncan looked at the note, then looked at me. "You waited to get this to me because … ?"

"Because for half a moment I forgot I was a strong, accomplished woman who doesn't need to hide things from her husband or the police."

Duncan gave me a look that said hiding things from the police was a bad idea and he was ready to let me have it, so I hurriedly threw myself on my sword. "I'm really very sorry. I promised Cal that I will come to you guys immediately with any other notes or … well, anything."

That took the wind out of his sail. "Fine."

He studied the note another minute and then asked, "Do you have any idea who might have put this in your pocket?"

I shook my head. "No, I've been over it and over it again in my head, but I couldn't come up with anyone near me other than Cal."

"How about we come at it from a different angle, who did you see at the Halloween party who had access to the studio?"

I'd already made note of who I'd talked to. "Julie Iron is one of *Cereal Killers* costume designers. Ruthy Mann, runs a coffee stall at the studio. Cathy Walker, from *Dead Man Walking*. I'm pretty sure I saw Steve Cade, her partner, there, too. Normally Steve and Cathy are together. She had another woman from their set. A dialogue coach."

I'd never thought about the fact Cathy's last name was Walker and the show was *Dead Man Walking*. I wondered if it was on purpose. I decided it probably had more to do with zombies being dead and walking than Cathy's name.

"That's just who I remember talking to. So many people at the studio have kids at the school. I bet there were a lot more."

Duncan nodded. "Okay. I'll get a list of parents who have kids at school and then see who works at the studio. It will narrow down our focus."

"Will you keep me informed?" I asked.

He rolled his eyes. "Not very likely. But I will let you know if I have further questions."

"You make me miss Charlie," I groused.

Cal laughed. "I'm going to tell him you said that."

"Don't," I said quickly. "He'll get all full of himself and impossible to live with."

Baby cop didn't seem impressed by our banter.

"I'll be in touch," he said as he walked out of the room. I slumped into a chair. "So are you going to let me have it now."

"No. That would be very unseemly and not the least bit professional. But I will let you *have it* tonight." He wiggled his eyebrows and I realized we were talking about having two very different things.

"I really am sorry, Cal."

"Quince, I know this has messed you up more than you've admitted. You're not thinking straight. So I forgive you. Just remember next time that you can come to me with anything."

I got up and kissed him again. "I know that wasn't professional, but sometimes a girl's gotta do what a girl's gotta do. We'll discuss you letting me *have it* tonight after Hank's in bed."

He smiled. "I can't wait."

I felt a million times lighter as I walked out of the police station. I was daydreaming about my evening when I practically ran into Charlie.

"Hey, you," I said about my old nemesis turned friend.

"Hey yourself. How're things?" he asked.

I was pretty sure he liked me more now that he wasn't directly involved in investigating a crime I was investigating.

"Someone doesn't want me talking to anyone about the dead zombie." I knew the zombie had a name, but it seemed less painful to refer to him as a zombie than as Brad Michna.

"Quincy, did you tell—"

I interrupted him. "I told Cal and Duncan. I almost didn't but the guilt got to me."

"And Cal warned you about staying out of it?" he asked, warning me to stay out of it with just his tone.

I realized he hadn't. "No."

"Quincy…" He sighed.

It was the same sort of sigh I expected Cal to give me.

"I'm not investigating, Charlie. I just asked a few questions. I'm trusting you guys to get to the bottom of it."

"I hate that we had to pass you off to Duncan. Don't get me wrong, he's a good detective, one of my best, but…"

"But I'm married to Cal, and you're like my big brother. I understand. I tripped over the body. I'm in this like it or not, so you can't be in it. It's okay, Charlie."

"Don't go getting into trouble, okay?" he said softly and more big-brotherly than coply. "I'm older now. I don't think my heart can stand it."

I smiled. "I'll behave."

I felt better than I'd felt since I landed on a zombie. I texted Dick. "*Meet me at Big G's. I'm starving.*"

CHAPTER SEVEN

When I'd first met Big G., I'd thought he didn't look nearly as big as his nickname implied he was. He was average height and had greying hair then. Now, it was practically white. Not as white as Steve's, but close.

Big G had mentioned a few visits back he blamed me for its lack of color. You'd think that would have annoyed me, but truth be told, he'd offered to break me out of jail in the past, and he was an amazing cook, so no offense was taken.

Yes, I can be bought by good food.

"Quincy, my love. Are you ready to leave Cal for a real man?" Big G. waggled his eyebrows at me.

"I think my husband and your wife would be annoyed if I did."

Big G. had married my friend Honey. They'd met because of me. I claimed it gave me some matchmaker street creds.

No one else seemed to buy it though.

"Yeah, I guess Honey might be upset. I mean, losing a man like me would devastate her." He literally patted himself on the shoulder.

I snorted. "How's Trixie?"

"Amazing."

Trixie was Honey's daughter, but you wouldn't Trixie wasn't Big G's as well. They were father-and-daughter close.

"Dick's waiting for you at your table," he said. "Know what you want?"

"Whatever you bring me," I said, giving my standard answer. He'd never let me down.

He smiled. "Good call."

I went to *my* table and found Dick already digging into a huge antipasto.

"I've been thinking about the show…" he started but his excitement faded before his words caught up and stopped as well. "What happened with Cal?"

I told him. "He didn't tell me to stay out of it. He even cut me some slack about not showing him the note right away."

Dick nodded. "He loves you. You have to remember that."

I nodded.

"Maybe we need a list of who you actually spoke to?" Dick said.

"Of course, I'll share it with Duncan and Cal," I said, nodding. I still felt guilty about not showing Cal the note immediately. "I've been thinking about it since I talked to them. It would really narrow the suspect pool, but think about it, Hollywood is really just a small town. I'm sure everyone working on *Dead Man Walking* knows I was just there. Everyone on our set knows I was talking to them and the *Dead* cast. Everyone knows. And that means the killer knows… Really even if I wouldn't know them from Adam, they know I'm looking."

He sighed. "Yeah. You didn't know Willy at the Bit Part Bar. He wasn't even someone on your list. And of course, the killer on *Cereal Killers* surprised everyone…including us," he acknowledged.

We'd had two characters who could have done it, in mind as we worked our way through the series. We left all kinds of clues about both. But we weren't sure until the beginning of this season which one we'd actually make the murderer. We set it up made it so either would work. Both of us thought keeping some sense of ambiguity made for better television.

"Yeah, our pool is still as big," Dick said.

I shook my head. "I'm going to try and stay out of it. I'm going to be a grandmother. I don't want to take any risks, and if someone's already annoyed…" I let the sentence trail of. "No, I'm staying out of it. I took the note to Cal and we gave it to Duncan." I added, "Of course, if we stumble over anything, I'll say something."

"See something, say something." Dick's smile said he didn't really believe I'd manage to stay out of it.

I nodded, assuring both him and myself that I meant what I said.

"His funeral is tomorrow," Dick blurted out.

"Whose?" I asked, wondering where Big G. was with my food. Despite Pattycake's pancakes, I was starving.

Confessions made me hungry.

"Michna's."

I shook my head. "It's been a month. Who has a funeral after a month?"

Dick shook his head. "I heard there was the issue of the autopsy. And his kid was on a walk-about."

"A walk-about?" I asked.

"That's what Murphy called it—he was on some spiritual retreat in Tibet or some place like that. And since no one else really cared, they waited for him to come back for the funeral. Murphy said he'd be amazed if anyone but the kid showed up."

Murphy had moved into Dick's six months ago. He'd used the phrase *Murphy said* a lot since then. Murph worked on a reality show *Stranded*—a group of people were literally stranded at some remote location for months. I was pretty sure I'd never submit my name for something like that. Unless I had restaurants nearby, I wasn't interested in going. But Murph loved it and was gone for months at a time. I always knew when he was in town because *Murphysaid* popped up more.

"Murphy said," Dick said, which made me smile, "that Michna did some work on *Stranded* for a season. He was well liked. No one put it together that he was the host of *Behind the Scenes*. I've got to think he's not nearly as popular now. He did a dug up dirt on a lot of shows and celebrities."

"So Murphy's a suspect, too?" I teased.

Dick laughed. "It was before his time on the show, but it was all the crew talked about after they heard. No one was mourning Michna's death."

There it was.

I felt bad.

Michna might have dissed me and my show, but it didn't seem right that no one would mourn him.

"We could go scope the funeral out and see if anyone else turns up," Dick said.

I shook my head. "No. I meant it. I'm out of the investigation. I might write about amateur detectives for television, but I know I'm not one. I was thrust into my other cases. I'm staying out of this one."

When I got home today, I was retiring my whiteboard permanently.

"Really?" Dick asked.

"Really. I'm done."

I'd leave it to Cal's buddies on the police force. They dealt with murders and other crimes every day. They could handle one dead-dead zombie.

I was out of it.

I was back in it.

I didn't know I was back in it when I woke up.

As a matter of fact, the next morning started out like most days.

Cal rushed out of the house with some call and Hank did the opposite of rushing. He dawdled.

I had a rule...three times and you're out. So the third time I called him to get up and get ready for school and he ignored me, I pulled the pillow from beneath his head and unceremoniously pulled the sheet off his bed, exposing his plaid boxer covered butt. I swatted it with the pillow.

"Twenty minutes. I will be in the car, leaving to take you to school in twenty minutes. You'll be there as well, dressed or not. I'm sure going to school in plaid boxers is your idea of a good time, right?"

"Mooooommmmmm," he groaned, still half asleep.

"Nineteen minutes."

I left the room and quickly broke into my stash of cinnamon Poptarts and grabbed a pint of milk, putting both in my purse.

We were both in the car precisely on time.

"I hope you're happy," he grumbled. "I'm going to starve today."

"I highly doubt skipping one breakfast will lead to starvation," I said with perfectly pitched mom-snark. Then I relented and said, "Look in my purse."

Hank did. "You're the best." He smiled at me and reminded me so much of Cal it floored me. I'd grown accustomed to the idea that the other boys were adults. I missed them when they were gone, but I was thrilled they'd all grown into self-supporting adults.

More than that, I was in awe of the men they'd become.

But Hank? He was my baby. But in that one Cal-glance, I'd seen the man he'd someday be and ached at the thought. I halfway missed the adult Hank, even though the little boy was still sitting next to me.

I knew he wouldn't welcome my insight, so I mom-snarked him again, "No, if I were the best we wouldn't be having such a rough morning. You're too old for this nonsense."

Too-old reminded me that he was almost halfway to adulthood and I squelched my sigh.

"Sorry," he said. "I only had twenty pages left on my book last night and thought I could finish them quicker than I did. I got to sleep kind of late."

And that is how a righteously indignant mother turns into a mushy puddle on the floor mat of her car.

"Did you finish?" I asked.

"Yeah. It was good," he said between a mouthful of Poptart.

"Next time maybe leave off until morning."

"Ah, Mom." In those two words he said *you'll never understand me.*

As far as excuses went, staying up reading was a great excuse for getting up late.

I pulled up in front of the school and made my escape before Adrienne could make her way to my car and ask me to work on some other project.

Rather than heading home or meeting Dick to work on the new proposal, I found myself heading to a funeral home. I'd been thinking about it, chasing the idea around and around in my head. I'm not sure when I finally settled on a decision, but before I knew it I was on my way to Homer's Funeral Home.

I had an immediate vision of Homer Simpson in my mind. Homer as an unfortunate mortician.

There were only two cars in the parking lot.

I checked my watch. It was ten thirty. The service started at eleven.

I felt worse.

Everyone should have someone to mourn them.

I was glad I decided to go with black slacks and a black and grey blouse. I looked suitably mourny.

I hadn't mentioned I was coming to the funeral home to Cal because I didn't want him to think I was still asking question about Michna. That's not why I was here.

I figured if you found yourself on top of a man—a dead man—no matter what the circumstances, you should show up at his funeral.

I walked into the funeral home. A man in a black suit and an Addam's Family expression pointed to the viewing room to the left.

I took a deep breath and went in. There was a casket at the far end of the small room, along with a few chairs and couches and a single row of folding chairs in front of the casket.

There weren't any flowers.

I don't think I'd ever gone to a funeral with no flowers at all.

There were only three people present—a younger man who was maybe in his mid-twenties, a dark-haired, older man in an expensive suit who had reached that age where men sort of stayed, somewhere between forty and the rest of their life. And there was a beautiful, stunning actually, blonde woman. Age-wise, she had to be somewhere between the other two men.

All three of them turned and looked at me as I came in. I felt very conspicuous. I figured I'd blend into the crowd and no one would notice me. It's hard to blend in a "crowd" of four…counting me.

The younger man came over. "Hi, I'm Brad's son, Tony. And you are?"

Yeah, Quincy. Good thinking.

How are you going to explain that you're the woman who discovered this boy's father's corpse…by falling on it?

"I work at the studios. I didn't really know your dad, but I felt like I should be here."

"You're the only one," Tony said bitterly. "I know he did stories about Hollywood on his podcast, but it wasn't like that was some internationally acclaimed broadcast. I think at his best, he had fifteen thousand listeners. He couldn't really hurt anyone."

And I felt guilty not for just tripping over him, but for being so upset when Michna had done his piece on me. "I'm sorry no one else showed up."

Tony shrugged as if it didn't matter, but I was mom enough to see it did. It was everything I could do not to sweep this hurting kid into my arms and mom hug him. Instead, I reached out and put my hand on his shoulder. "I really am sorry."

He tried to shrug it off. "It's fine."

The other two meandered over and I realized Tony looked a lot like the older guy. He must be a relative. "Emmy and Uncle Barry, this is…"

"Quincy," I filled in.

He nodded. "She works at the studio."

Emmy grimaced. "You're the one that fell over Brad?" she asked.

The problem with a name like Quincy is you're generally the only one in any given situation.

She laughed. "Well, at least Brad went out the way he lived ... with a woman on top of him."

She turned and walked away from me with "Uncle Barry" hot on her heels.

"Sorry," Tony said. "Dad cheated on her again. To hear her tell it, with some little pink haired floozy. He treated her horribly. I'm not sure their marriage would have lasted much longer."

Jilted wife kills cheating husband in order to inherit everything rather than split their assets?

No, I scolded myself. I was out of this investigation. I was going to leave it to the cops. I'm sure Duncan had thought of that angle. And he'd probably asked himself how Emmy would have gotten access to the studio, just like I was asking myself right now.

"I'm so sorry. I didn't want to say that I was the one who found him ... tripped over him ..." I shook my head. There was no good way to finish that sentence. "I'm sorry."

"Thanks for coming. That must have been horrible for you."

"It was. Losing your father must be hard on you as well. It's kind of you to think about me."

He shook his head. "Losing my father should be horrible. It should cut me to the core. But between you and me, we were never close. He divorced my mom when I was ten. He treated her as badly as he treated Emmy. I saw him every few months, but we never got along. He never understood me. I teach theology. I was at a retreat in Tibet when he died. No one could reach me, which is why the funeral's so late."

His voice broke, belying his idea that his father's death left him unaffected.

He got himself under control and said, "I feel so guilty and torn. I know I should be devastated, but losing my father will barely make a ripple in my life. I hadn't talked to him since one night last summer when I called to tell him I'd be gone for a few months. He asked me when I was going to get a real job."

He shrugged. "What do I do with that?"

"He was your father. He might have been a perfect man." That was an understatement. He sounded horrible. "He might not have understood you, and you might not have understood him, but you were connected. You stayed in contact with him enough to let him know you'd be gone. He cared enough to want you to have a real job. I know it's not the kind of caring you wanted, but it was a type of caring nonetheless. I always figured you have to simply accept people the way they are and not mourn the way you wish they were. He was your dad. You were his son. He's gone. It's okay to hurt."

I didn't have to think about hugging Tony—this young man who reminded me so much of my boys—this time, because he hugged me.

"Thank you," he said. "I deal with philosophy, and I've heard that said different ways, but your way made sense."

"I'm glad."

Tony pulled me into the chair next to him when the minister arrived. His stepmother and uncle sat next to us.

It was a quick service.

Afterward, I hugged the sad young man again. "You remind me of my sons."

"How many do you have?" he asked.

"Four. I have to get back to pick the youngest up at school. But it was nice to meet you, despite the circumstances."

"Thanks for listening." Other than sitting in the same row during the funeral, his uncle and stepmother stayed out of his vicinity. "It was hard feeling I was all alone here."

I dug in my mom-bag and pulled out a card, not sure why I was offering it, but sure that I should. "Here's my number. If you need someone, call."

He took it, reached in his pocket and pulled out one and handed it to me as well. "Thank you, Quincy."

"I am really sorry for your loss."

I hurried out of the funeral home and drove across town to pick up Hank.

I couldn't help but think how much Tony's relationship with his father echoed mine with my mother when I was young. I didn't feel she understood me, and when she expressed her concerns, it felt like her judging me, not caring about me.

Over the years I'd learned that sometimes a relationship wasn't built on reality, but rather on perception.

When I looked at Mom from a new perspective, our relationship gradually shifted. We were very different people, but we'd found common ground in the fact we were both fiercely in love with our kids. My mother would do anything for me. It took me a while to recognize that.

I was struck with a wave of sadness that Tony and his father would never have an opportunity to come to terms like that.

I was a bit misty as Hank crawled in the car. He began his after-school litany as we headed home. "...and Mom, Caesar farted so loud. The whole cafeteria looked and he bowed, Mom. He just bowed. The smell was deadly. Miss Taylor sent him to the bathroom, but he said he didn't have to go, but she looked like she was going to barf and told him to go and try to go to the bathroom anyways. And then..."

I was not a perfect mother. But these were the moments I tried to save up and store. Moment when Hank shared his day with me. Moments when the older boys called just to talk.

A grandmother.

I'd been so caught up in my zombie fall that I don't think I'd really let the fact that I was going to be a grandmother really sink in.

There would be someone else in the car someday sharing stories of their day with me. He or she would prattle away and I would store up all those words with joy.

I'd tell Eli and LeeAnn to store them up as well. One moment my boys were Hank's age, talking about a friend's farts, and the next they were coming home and telling me I was going to be a grandmother.

"Mom, are you crying? I'm sorry it was a B. I'll work hard and study more before the next test. I can read any word the teacher gives me, but spelling doesn't make sense. But I'll study more and—"

"Honey, it wasn't your test. It was the fact you're getting so old. Next thing you know, you'll be heading off to college and I'll miss you."

"Oh. I won't go far. Me and Caesar are gonna be roommates but we don't like to cook, so we're going somewhere close to home so you and Aunt Tiny can cook for us. And you'll call and ask if I want to go see Aunt Honey and Big G and I'll say yes." I glanced in the rearview mirror at Hank's rapturous expression. "We can't cook, but we do like to eat."

I was laughing as we pulled into the driveway and when Hank walked around to my side of the car I pulled him into my arms and hugged him. He squirmed, but not too much.

"I will cook for you and Caesar when you're in college. I mean, if you get hungry, then you'll come over and I'll get to see you a lot. It'll be almost like you never left home."

Hank wiggled out of my hug and headed for the door.

My heart was overflowing with love for Hank, for his brothers, for LeeAnn, and the new baby, for Cal—always Cal—for my family…

"Mom," Hank cried in such a way I knew something was wrong.

There on my front door was a doll that was meant to look like a zombie. Oh, it wasn't done well. I couldn't be sure but it looked like magic markers were the primary decorating material.

There was a note that said, *LAST WARNING.*

The note was stuck to the zombie with a knife that pinned it to the door.

"Don't touch anything. Go back and get in the car and lock it while I call your dad."

I didn't touch anything either. I called Cal and had him bring the reinforcements.

But I did take a picture with my cellphone.

I was back in this.

No one messes with my family, especially my kids.

No zombie murdering murderer…well, as a writer, I knew that was redundant, but I also knew I wouldn't rest until whoever killed Brad Michna was behind bars.

I called Tiny, too. I asked her to come get Hank. Someone knew where I lived and I didn't want him to be here.

Cal and Duncan arrived together in the same car. Cal was driving.

I don't know why I noticed that, but I did. And I noticed it seemed to take him an inordinately long time to walk over to me. Hank got out of the car and ran to his dad. "There's a stabbed zombie on the door, Dad. It's so cool. You'll figure out who did it, right?"

Hank looked at me. "I'm gonna be a detective like you and dad. Me and Caesar are gonna start our own agency. When I get really good cases, I'll tell you and you and Uncle Dick can write stories about them and…"

Tiny pulled up as Hank continued his word vomit.

"Come on Hank," I said.

"But Mom, I want to stay and watch Dad and that other guy solve the case. Me and Caesar need to start learning now so we can be the best."

"We'll tell you all about it later," I promised. "Right now, you go home with Aunt Tiny."

He sighed.

"Just a minute," I said to Cal and Duncan. I led Hank to the car. "I'll call later," I promised.

She just nodded and said, "Get in and buckle up, Buddy."

I headed back. Cal and Duncan were standing in front of the door studying the zombie doll.

"What did you do today?" Duncan asked. "Were you home?"

"I wasn't home most of the day," I admitted. "I went to Brad Michna's funeral and—"

"I thought you were staying out of this?" Cal said, sounding angry.

I like to think that I'm a pretty mellow person, but after all these years, Cal should have known better than talking to me in that tone of voice.

"I was staying out of it, Cal. The funeral wasn't an in-it thing, it was a human thing. Michna was killed in my writers' room. How could I not go pay my respects?"

"You were probably casing the funeral for suspects," Duncan said, snarkily.

"I wasn't because I was staying out of this," I said more snippily than I'd responded to Cal. I loved Cal, but at the moment, I was pretty sure Duncan didn't even hit my like-list. "But if that was a plausible avenue of investigation, why didn't I see you there?"

That stopped him. He stuttered, "I, I, I—"

I interrupted. "I'll confess, I'm not feeling overly confident in your abilities at the moment."

Okay, so that was even snarkier than he'd been, but seriously, I had kids older than this man-child who was trying to scold me. "And in case Cal didn't tell you, I don't lie. Oh, I sometimes don't tell someone everything, but if I do tell you something, you can bet it's the truth. So here's the truth, I went to the funeral because I was the one who found the body. Dick mentioned it as part of an investigation, but I wasn't part of that. Still I couldn't let go of the notion. Mr. Michna deserved at least that much from me. Turns out, he didn't have many friends. His brother was there, his wife—who he was thinking about divorcing and cheated on—and his son."

"I'll check into them." Duncan paused a moment and said, "I'm sorry I accused you of lying."

He looked as if he meant it, so I nodded and said, "Apology accepted."

Duncan went to work bagging the zombie doll and knife. There was a hole in my door from the knife. It was a tangible reminder that my home had been violated. As if he could read my mind, Cal put an arm over my shoulder. "It's going to be okay, Quince."

That's what he said, but I wasn't the only one who occasionally omitted something. What he didn't say was he was pissed and he was frightened for me. What he didn't say was he loved me.

He didn't need to. I knew it.

And I was sure he knew that I loved him, too. But I'd make sure later.

When Duncan finished, he took the zombie and knife with him and left.

Cal looked at me with the intensity I imagined he used when interrogating suspects. I imagined it intimidated most of them. Unfortunately for Cal, I was his wife and nothing he could do would intimidate me.

"You weren't in it when you went to the funeral, but now...?" he left the question hanging.

I didn't need to answer because he just nodded and said, "Let's get out your whiteboard again."

My heart constricted with love. "I love you, you know that, right?" I checked.

He wrapped his arm around me. "Of course you do, how could you not?" he teased.

We got out the whiteboard and I made arrangements for Hank to stay with Caesar for a few nights. Tiny said, "Quincy, don't do anything crazy."

"I won't. Cal is in this too."

"Okay. But if you need a lawyer, you know where to call."

"I do. I think you marrying Sal was one of the best ideas you ever had."

She laughed, though it sounded a bit forced. "I'll tell him you said so. Be careful."

"I will," I promised.

By the time I was done, Cal was already writing on the board.

And I realized *I* wasn't in it...

We were in it.

Cal and I had lists.

One that included specific people Michna had done hit podcasts on.

It was a long list. In fairness, I was on it.

Then we added his family. His wife, his brother, and—regretfully—I added his son.

I started digging.

Tony Michna was an associate professor. A very young one. But from comments online, a popular one with the girls.

I wondered how far the apple fell from the proverbial tree?

He had indeed been overseas, according to the school's news.

Michna's brother, Barry, was virtually non-existent online. He didn't have a Facebook page, or a Twitter page. Nothing in the paper. Nothing in a generic search, other than showing up in Michna's obituary. *"Survived by his older brother, Barry."*

I kept digging and finally found him listed as a Cougar Point College graduate with a degree in business.

I walked to the whiteboard and stared at my list.

Tony
Barry
Emmy

Those were my top tier because everyone knows spouses and family members are the top suspects in a murder. I guess no one can love you or hate you as much as family. It was kind of sad.

Then I started listing people from around the studio.

Cathy Walker
Steve Cade

I added the director that week and a few of the other cast members who'd Michna's podcast had mentioned.

In fairness, I added my name and Dick's. I put in our casts' names, then our crew. Poor Soho Morning was our director that week. I didn't think she'd done it, but until I could rule her out, I'd leave her.

Then I started crossing off cast and crew who'd never been mentioned on Michna's podcast. Some just because I couldn't see it. I mean, really, Mrs. Kelly was eighty if she was a day. She could still sew a mean stitch, but I couldn't see her shooting someone in the head.

There were others like her I just crossed off. I wasn't a cop. I didn't need a detailed and verified alibi. I could trust my gut.

I'd worked on a murder mystery show for years.

In a weird way, death had become my life.

Oh, wow, that was good. I wondered if Dick and I could use that as a tagline for something?

I jotted it in the corner of the white-board.

Dick and I knew that obvious killers were frequently the killers, but good television meant throwing in some twists—killers who viewers never saw coming. But in real life, there was more logic to it. Killers had motives. They had to have opportunity. And even the ability. Kathi Kelly didn't have the ability.

So I crossed her off because I didn't think she could have done it.

I also didn't think it could be people like BJ Lynn, Jaynce Al'Caren, Helen Lorelei, Georgia Peach (yes, for real, that was her name... I asked once if that was the name on her birth certificate and it was), Tricia Tami (not the name on her birth certificate and I had no idea why she'd go with that) and...

Well, I just started running lines through names because no matter how my writer's brain twisted it, they didn't merit consideration. That was another thing I'd learned, most reasons for killing someone are pretty basic. Things like jealousy, anger, greed, revenge, money, domestic related...

A lot of people had a reason to be angry with Michna. Fewer fell into the other categories.

I needed to talk to his family again.

I'd chatted with Tony at the funeral home. Maybe it was time to talk to his wife and his brother.

What sort of reason could I invent to go see either of them?

"Quincy, what are you thinking?" Cal asked.

I'd almost forgotten he was here. I'd fallen into the zone. Dick and I did it all the time when we were working. If I was quiet, he let me be, and vice versa.

"Sorry. I was thinking this isn't exactly the way Duncan would approach a suspect list, but I know so many of these people. People like Deb just couldn't have done it. She's tiny and sweet. Her nickname is Bubbles. Sprites don't kill."

"Quincy, you know better than that. Real investigation can't be based on a gut feeling. Facts. Proof. Those are things a real detective needs," Cal said, as if he were lecturing new recruits.

"Well, there you go. I am not a real detective, I might write them for television, but I know the difference. I'm sure Duncan is going to cross all the evidence T's and dot all the alibi I's. And while fact and fiction are two very different things, there is a certain element of truth to any fiction. If there's not, then the viewers won't buy it."

Cal sighed. "Fine. You look at this however you need to. So tell me what you're thinking."

"If I were writing about a dead zombie—"

"Zombies are inherently dead," Cal quipped, going back to what was become standard humor in our house.

I couldn't help but grin though. "Funny. Maybe you should leave the comedy to me and Eli? A dead-dead zombie."

He laughed. "Sorry. Go on."

"So if I were writing this, I'd look at family first, but they don't have access to the studio, so I think I'd turn my attention to people who do. I'd talk to the family, but I don't think they're the ones. They might say something that helps though. I really think it's got to be someone who has access to the studio. I've asked around, but given the zombie on the door, that isn't working very well."

"So what are we going to do?" he asked.

I took his hand. I loved every *we* he said.

"I think I'm going to need to spread the word that I'm not investigating. That I'm so traumatized about what happened, I'm staying as far away from zombie investigations as I can get. I'll talk to people at the studio, not as someone investigating anything, but as someone who's broken up about falling on a zombie. And I think I'm going to mention not wanting to investigate because someone's leaving threatening notes."

Cal quirked his eyebrows. I didn't know how else to describe that expression, but I totally understood him.

We'd once tried to get James Stone, who played Ajax on *Cereal Killer* to make that expression, but he couldn't do it. I knew that when Cal did it, it meant he was thinking.

Finally he said, "I don't see the logic there."

"Well, if I'm not investigating, just working through my trauma with friends, I'm not a threat to the murderer and I'm technically following their zombie voodoo doll instructions. But people might tell poor traumatized Quincy something you and Duncan can use it. Plus, people there know me after all these years. They'll be more relaxed than if they were talking to the cops. I don't see how I can take you and make it look legit."

"So you want me to let you investigate on your own?"

I shook my head. "No, I want you to let me talk to friends about my trauma and see if I can find any information Duncan can use."

"It could be dangerous," he said quietly.

I squeezed his hand. "I'm actually doing this to be make things safer. To convince the murderer their voodoo zombie worked."

I understood him worrying. Most days I didn't say to myself that Cal was going out to investigate murder, though that was what he was doing. I simply told myself he was going to work. It made me worry less to think about him at work.

"I'm actually trying to make myself safer," I said.

"And you won't be alone with anyone?" he asked.

"No. No private office meetings. I'll make sure I'm in view of people all the time, I promise." I meant it. I had a great life. I wasn't going to put myself at risk for this.

"And you'll be assuring people you're just too traumatized to look into this?" he asked again.

I nodded.

"As much as I hate to admit it, that is a solid plan. It might get whoever is sending you these messages off your back. And people at the studio will be more inclined to say something to you. Duncan's talked to people on both sets, but said he's made very little headway."

"I might be able to help. I don't want to solve anything. I really did just go to the funeral because it was a human thing to do. I was happily out of it until the note and the zombie voodoo doll. I just want this finished so I can get back to the life we've built and I can get down to enjoying my new grandbaby."

Cal gave me a platonic kiss. "I hate that you're right, but if you're just talking to friends, not investigating, you might get info we'd never have a chance at getting."

"Then I'm on it."

"Just be careful," he warned.

"I will," I promised. Then I realized that with Hank at Tiny's there was only me and Cal in the house.

I kissed him back … and it wasn't platonic in the least.

CHAPTER EIGHT

Maybe I should have been an actress after all.

I mean, all those years ago, I came to Hollywood to act. Then my ex happened, and then the boys, and then I went into business with Tiny, and then I meet Cal, and then I started writing and...

I built a good life.

But maybe I should have kept acting because...I was amazing.

I went to the studio under the guise of having a meeting.

That wasn't a lie exactly. I'd learned when writing fiction that sticking as close to the truth as possible made for a better lie. This time, I did have a meeting with Joanne Podarski. She was one of the producers for *Cereal Killers*. We'd named one of the moms after her...we never admitted that though. We let her think it was a coincidence.

Joanne and I talked about our new idea and she seemed enthused.

"So how are you doing?" she asked, all sympathy. It was weird, to be honest. Joanne was all business, all the time. Concern from her was disconcerting, but I remembered my goal. I decided to use Joanne as my shaky and vulnerable dry run before going out in public.

"I'm fine." My voice actually quavered.

I hesitantly added, "It's tough though, you know. The studio used to feel like home. I felt safe. Now..." I left the sentence hang and bowed my head, brushing a hand against my eyes.

Seriously, I totally rocked at shaky-vulnerable.

Joanne slid her chair closer and patted my shoulder.

It was the most human display of emotion I'd ever seen her make. "I'm so sorry you have to go through this again, Quincy. Do you have any ideas who did it?"

I shook my head. "No, I'm staying of it. I mean, I'm staying so far out of it I'm not even thinking about it. There's a younger detective looking into things. Cal says he's good."

Joanne nodded. "We've seen him around the studio. He's been poking around and talking to people. They want him to release the *Cereal Killers'* set, but he won't."

I didn't have to ask who *they* was. *They* was—were—the Studio powers that be. *They* didn't like things vacant and unused.

"That's good to hear," I said. "I don't want to deal with any of this. Dick and I are working on our pitch for the new series."

She nodded again. "Did the detective tell you when he's going to release the set? They don't have the crime scene tape up anymore, but he doesn't want to release the set. I don't know what he thinks he's going to find there. The murder didn't happen on set."

I shook my head. "I don't know. He hasn't told me anything." I decided to pile it on. "He's concerned, you know. I mean, yesterday someone left a voodoo zombie on my door as a warning. I'm terrified all the time. I couldn't be of any help with this case if I wanted to be. And I don't want to be."

Joanne gave me an odd look. Was she it? Was she the murderer? Suddenly *shaky and vulnerable* didn't seem like much of a stretch. Everyone who worked here was a suspect. All the people I knew and worked with might have done it. Any of them could have left me those warnings.

I didn't feel I was rocking at acting any more. "I just want this to be over," I said. And I did.

"Oh, Quincy, I'm so sorry you're going through this."

"Me, too," I assured her.

I wanted to go back to my normal life.

"Well, you let us know if there's anything you need, okay?" Joanne said, still weirdly human.

I wasn't sure who us was—maybe it was the powers-that-be and Joanne?—but I nodded. "I will, Joanne. Thanks."

I tried not to smile as I left her office and headed to my set … my old set.

I was an actress.

An actress who wanted to find the murderer so she could get back to her life.

It was weird to find the set so quiet.

Someone with access to the studio had killed Michna.

Which meant it was someone I knew.

Someone who didn't want me looking into things.

The thoughts kept circling around and around in my head.

Maybe that's why I didn't notice immediately I wasn't alone. To say I was surprise to see baby detective standing in the center of the stage was an understatement. I stifled a small scream when I saw him standing there.

My first thought was, *the murderer's here for me.*

I tried to cover my fright up and sound nonchalant as I said, "Hi, Duncan."

I thought I'd managed it and once again felt pretty good about my acting skills. Yes, I'd sounded almost normal.

His eyes narrowed. "What are you doing here?"

"I had a few meetings today." Again, not really a lie. I met with Joanne and was heading over the see Cathy at *Dead Man Walking*. "I'll confess, everything seems different. Everyone seems different. I look at these people I know and work with and wonder, did this one or that one do it?" I shook my head. "What are you doing here?"

"We're releasing the set and crime scene," he said.

"Joanne was just talking about that. The studio will be happy."

Duncan looked anything but happy. "We've got all the evidence out of the writer's room. The crime scene guys have been over it with a fine tooth comb."

"Our producer said you didn't want to release the actual set either?"

Duncan shrugged. The gesture and his expression reminded me of Hank. "We didn't find the gun, and I wondered if someone stashed it in here. There are a lot of places to hide a gun."

"You let us finish shooting in here," I pointed out.

I might not be a cop, but it seemed to me if he thought there was a murder weapon lying around, he shouldn't have.

"It's not a crime scene per se, but still…" He shrugged again.

"Still you wonder if someone stashed something in here?" I looked around. If I were the murderer where would I hide the gun?

"Yes," Duncan said. "You've got a ton of places to hide things. We've been through it, but before I release the set, I wanted to take one more look."

"So you're looking for someplace where a gun could be hidden, or even the clothes the murderer was wearing could have been stashed? I mean, it was messy in there. They could have gotten," I was thinking blood or brains, but I said, "stuff on their shirts."

"Yes," he muttered.

"Although, with a zombie show next door, it's not unusual to see zombies, and blood and gut covered actors walking around. Of course, if it isn't an actor, we're back to it looking suspicious."

He paused and looked at me funny. "Valid points. Keep talking."

"Pardon?" I said.

"You're thinking out loud," he said. "And it's helpful."

I laughed. "I'm used to working with Dick, my writing partner. We think out loud on a regular basis. I come up with an idea, he tweaks it. I shoot it down, he comes up with something else." I don't know that I even considered how lucky I was to work with someone who liked my stream of consciousness rambles.

I smiled at Duncan. "Okay. So, I don't think the murderer could have been his son," I didn't mention that I didn't think that because I liked his son, "or family because they wouldn't have access to the studio and would stick out like a sore thumb wandering around here late at night."

He nodded. I walked to Beth's kitchen. Each kitchen was in a corner of the stage. The equipment filled up the middle and other side. I opened a drawer. Some opened, some didn't. "So it has to be someone with access to HeartMark studios, not necessarily someone who worked on my set, or next door."

"I'm still looking at the family," Duncan said.

This time I nodded as I shut the drawer and ran my finger across the counter. "That makes sense. If I were writing this for television, I'd have my heroine check to see if the family has any connections to the studio. Someone who would allow them to have access. But if not, like I said I think it would be difficult for them to wander around here unnoticed."

"I've gone through the visitors' list that day and nothing jumped out at me. None of them were here, at least not listed as themselves."

I nodded. "I think someone who worked here would be on my short list, though in actuality there are so many people that work here, it's a long list. Maybe the coroner will give you some clues about the murderer."

"The bullet came from below Michna. So someone who was on the ground, or even your table. I'm hoping ballistics comes in with more. Everything's running behind."

I could hear the frustration in his voice.

"Well knowing the bullet came from below him might help," I said. "You've gone through the prop room?" I asked.

"We had a team go through everything before we let you all back on set. It seemed like a logical place to hide a gun. You guys have a ton in your prop room." His tone sounded slightly accusatory.

"We're a murder mystery show, so of course there are guns. But have you walked through the prop room?"

He shook his head.

"Let's take a look."

We looked. Duncan went through every prop gun in the room, even though they'd already been looked at. We had a dozen.

Despite how realistic they looked, none were the murder weapon.

He looked pissed, annoyed, and upset all at once. "I have no reason not to release the set. It's been over a month."

"I wish I could come up with some awesome hiding place," I said. "I think someone would have stumbled upon a real gun during our last scenes."

He smiled. "Me, too."

"I should get going. I have a meeting." That wasn't really a lie, though I was walking the truth-line. I was meeting with Cathy and Steve, but it wasn't formal the way I'd made it sound.

He nodded. "Thanks. If you think of anyone who had access to your writers' room, let me know."

"I will. I want this solved as much as you do."

Maybe more, I thought but didn't say.

I walked over to Cathy and Steve's office, thinking about why someone commits murder. Dick and I went over the list of motives often.

Love.
Hate.
Secrets.
Passion.
Greed.
Revenge.
Mental Issues.
Sympathy.
To Protect...yourself or someone else.

Obviously it wasn't an all-inclusive list. I mean, love can include a bunch of motives, and frankly some of those can also fall under hate. Jealousy...it's a dual thing. Love and hate and fear all wrapped up into one thing.

Then you can add the idea that some of these are premeditated and some happenstance.

Whether Michna was killed in my writers' room by accident would be a very different than if someone led him there to die because of...well, me.

If this were an episode of *Murder She Wrote*, Jessica Fletcher would have found the killer by now.

I was deep in my Who-Killed-Brad-Michna thoughts when I practically flattened a woman.

"I'm so sorry. My head's in the clouds," I said as I stepped back and looked at a vaguely familiar face. It took me a second to come up with who she was … Cathy's friend. "Ann?"

She nodded. "Hi, Quincy."

She looked nervous.

"What are you doing here?" I asked, which only made her look more nervous.

"I'm the dialogue coach here."

"You have kids on the set?"

She nodded. "A couple. And a few adults who need a bit of help, too."

Any show with kids will have a dialogue coach who works with them, but most will work with adults as well. Sometimes they're not just a dialogue coach, but an acting coach as well, but most actors find taking directions from a dialogue coach easier than from an acting coach.

Adrienne on our set was both dialogue and acting coach, and frankly we couldn't manage without her.

Couldn't have.

Past tense.

I was hoping if Dick and my proposal went well, we could get most of the old gang back together on the new show.

"Is everything okay?" Ann asked, looking as if things were less than okay for her. If I knew her better, I'd ask, but I'd barely come up with her name.

I realized I'd zoned out again for a second.

When I was mulling, zoning was part of the process. Some people wouldn't have even noticed, but Ann was perceptive. It was a quality that probably made her good at her job.

"I'm fine. Just thinking about our pitch for a new project."

"You'll do great," Ann said. "We all loved *Cereal Killers.* Cathy's in her office."

"Great. Thanks."

I was not a cop, so again, I didn't have to play by the cop rulebook. I couldn't help but feel since Michna was working at *Dead Man Walking*, the murderer was tied here somehow. Did someone find out he was going to do one of his podcasts about this show?

Why would they want to murder him over that, though?

The no-such-thing-as-bad-press was a well-accepted Hollywood adage for good reason.

I thought about my list of reasons to murder.

A secret?

That was Michna's specialty. Find some dirt on a person or a show and then talk about it no his podcast.

I guess I was actually pretty lucky. He simply hadn't liked my show and felt the need to bring up the fact I was a maid—as if it might embarrass me.

It didn't. I was proud of Mac'Cleaners. And even now that I didn't work in the day-to-day aspects of our business, I was still proud of what Tiny and I had built.

I'd raised the three older boys on that business.

It was good, honest work.

And that work had led me to this work.

I owed so much to Mac'Cleaners.

But what if someone at *Dead Man Walking* had a secret they weren't proud of?

Thoughts of secrets, murderers, and murder weapons danced through my head as I knocked on Cathy's door.

"Come in," she hollered. She smiled when she saw it was me. "How are you, my lovely friend?" she asked in her clipped English accent. "Steve and I are worried about you. Basically we're planning on being worried right up until they find out who Mr. Michna's murderer is. It is very disconcerting thinking someone on set or at the studio might have killed the man."

She laughed in a classic Cathy way. "Of course, to most people the fact I work with death for a living would make that statement sound absurd, but you get it, right?"

I nodded. "I do get it. I came over to check on you."

"Oh, aren't you lovely."

I'd teased Cathy and Steve about their British "lovelies" years ago. That only made them use the word more around me, and I found myself joining in the game.

I referred to them as my lovely friends and they returned the favor. "You know I think you and Steve are two of the loveliest people around."

"Don't tell him, but I think he's pretty smashingly lovely as well. He only has one tiny flaw." She held up one finger.

"What's that?" I asked.

She nodded for me to take a seat and poured me a cup of tea with a smile. She'd told me once that she might be in America, but she refused to bow to our uncivilized need for coffee. She generally had a pot of tea in her office in various stages of cooling.

Today's was hotter than lukewarm, which was good.

One day she'd served it to me so cold, I'd teased all it needed was ice cubes.

She'd informed me that iced tea was absolutely uncivilized.

I took a sip of my tea and smiled at the memory.

She continued her banter about Steve. "His one flaw is his love of opera. I've tried, Quincy. Goodness knows I've tried, but I just can't enjoy it. Give me a Broadway tune and I'm in heaven, but play an aria and I'm lost."

That was so Cathy-esque. Her idea of a flaw was endearing.

I smiled. "So what you're saying is opera is your version of sports? The boys and Cal keep trying to rope me into cheering for one sport team or another. I just pick Pennsylvania teams because it feels like it should. Steelers, Penguins, Pirates. I always cheer for them just to appease the family. I tend to cheer as they watch and I read a book."

I was not sporty. I'd never be sporty. But I did really support "my" teams. You could take the girl out of Western Pennsylvania, but you couldn't take Western Pennsylvania out of the girl.

Once a friend asked if I cheered for the Flyers and I was either sporty enough, or Western Pennsylvanian enough to snort my response. Now, I'm sure the Philadelphia Flyers were a lovely team... if you lived in Philly. But they weren't for me.

I needed to call my mom, I realized. I missed her.

"I think Steve would probably be annoyed if I read during an opera. I have gotten out of it a time or two by sending someone else with him." She chuckled. "He does love playing the teacher and is always hoping for new converts."

I chuckled. "You are devious."

"I am." She shot me a Cheshire Cat grin.

I took another sip of my tea. And Cathy asked, "Really, how are you doing?"

"The detective was here today. He says they're going to release the crime scene."

Now, I didn't for one second think that Cathy had killed Michna, but I did figure that people on her set were still talking about Michna and she might be just the person to tell them how distraught I was, so I put on my act.

"Did they find anything?" she asked.

I shook my head and carefully used the word *he* instead of *we*. "He went to the prop room and poked around. He figured if the killer was one of your zombie extras—" I said extras knowing Cathy wouldn't want to think of one her regular cast being the killer any more than I would—"they could get away with wearing bloody clothes, but maybe they'd be afraid to carry the murder weapon around the studio. The prop room seemed like a good place to stash it."

"Did he find anything?" she asked, picking up on my cue.

I shook my head, then bowed it down and blinked like crazy, hoping to manage a tear.

I was pretty sure my eyes looked shiny when I looked up at Cathy. "I wish he had. Someone left me a message, telling me to stay away from the investigation. I am. I'm terrified all the time. I just want this over."

She hugged me. "Someone is warning you off?" she muttered as she hugged me tighter. "Steve will be furious."

I wasn't sure Steve would be able to match Cathy's obvious fury.

"Thanks," I said.

"You know, if someone could have left evidence in your prop room, ours would be a good place too." She stood up. "Let's go check here."

"Really?" I asked.

"Yes. Frankly, we have a bunch more weapons than you guys do. Ours would be a safer bet. It takes a lot of guns to kill zombies—you shoot them in the head."

Cathy smiled, and again it struck me as incongruous that this happy, tea-drinking, English accented grandmother type worked for a zombie show.

"I don't think we should go search," I managed, putting on my act. Not that I thought the killer was Cathy, but because I wanted her talking about how upset I was to the cast and crew.

On the heels of that, I realized that shooting them in the head was exactly what the killer had done.

I shook my head and went back to playing my scene. "I've had threatening notes. I'm staying out of the investigation. I have too much to live for." On the heels of that thought, I realized that grandmotherly Cathy didn't know my big news.

"I'm going to be a grandmother," I blurted out. "That's what matters to me, not solving another mystery. I'm over the Maid in LA amateur detective shtick."

I gave a delicate shudder and Cathy hugged me. "I'm glad you're staying out of it. Let the cops do their job. You concentrate on the baby."

Everything in me wanted to go check that prop room with Cathy, but I didn't want to take any chances. "Maybe you should call the detective and offer to let him look through your prop room?"

"They did that once already, but you're right, it wouldn't hurt to have him look again."

I hung out for a while and talked to some of the cast as well as some of the crew. I thought I'd made a good start at spreading the Quincy's-not-investigating news. But I didn't feel as if I'd made any inroads in collecting clues.

But hopefully Cathy would say something to Steve and maybe they'd both mention how torn up I was to friends on the set.

It didn't take much for something like that to spread.

But still, I'd hoped for some useful bit of information.

So much for my insider access making me better able to investigate than Duncan or the other cops.

I decided to start back to our office, and as I walked over, I called Mom.

"Quincy, did you find anything new? I listened to the rest of Michna's podcasts. I sent you a list of names. Did you get it?" she asked.

Before I could answer, she said, "Your dad and I were talking. We really are going to buy a place. Something close, but not too close." She paused. "Did you call for something specific?"

This time she waited for me to answer.

"No. I was thinking about you and just called to say hi."

"No new clues?" she asked.

A crowd of people walked by and I answered a little more loudly than I normally would have, "No. I'm done with looking into this. The cops have it covered."

"As your mother, I'm relieved. As your co-investigator, I'm a bit disappointed. But when Dad and I move out there, we'll have plenty of time for investigations. Hopefully ones that don't involve murders. Maybe your next show?"

"Speaking of that," I said. "I wanted to ask you about killing someone off—"

"Should I be concerned?" There was amusement in her voice.

I laughed. "No. Dick and I were talking about our new show and need something dire for our priest to have."

"Well, you could try—"

She didn't get any further because I spotted Dick running toward me. "Here comes Dick. Can I call you back?"

"Sure, honey," my mom said. "I'll mull over deadly diseases."

"We need him dying, but coherent," I told her.

"Got it. Tell Dick I said hi."

As Dick reached me, I said, "Mom said hi. She's going to help us kill off the priest."

HOLLY JACOBS

"I was just heading to our office to tell you ... they loved
it," he said breathlessly.

"They who loved what?" I asked.

"TPTB," was our shorthand for The-Powers-That-Be,
"loved *Mass Murder*."

Dick generally took care of business. It worked out better that way. I wasn't sure if I'd known about today's meeting, but I felt a sense of relief as he continued, "They want
the first three scripts. With a two-hour premiere. And they
loved our first *Cereal Killer's* movie script. They're green
lighting that."

"So what you're saying is we're still employed." I
grinned.

"That's exactly what I'm saying." He stopped. "What are
you doing here?"

"I stopped to see Joanne, like we talked about. Then
bumped into baby cop. Duncan is releasing the crime
scene," I said. I wasn't really dodging his question, but I realized he might not be happy about me looking for insider
clues without him.

He grinned. "That's great because we're keeping the
stage for the movie, and then hopefully shooting *Mass
Murder* there, too."

A feeling of coming-home washed over me. I was already
thinking about calling back the cast and crew for the movie
and wondering if we could keep the crew on for *Mass Murder*
and ...

Dick looked at me closely and asked slowly, "What were
you doing again?"

"After I got done with Duncan, I visited with Cathy."

"Quincy, you were investigating, weren't you? Without
me?" I realized how right I'd been. There was a combina-
tion of accusation and disappointment in his expression.

"No, not really," I said quickly. "I ran into Duncan and then went to see Cathy and see if she'd thought of anything else."

Dick glowered in my direction. Though he'd built a career around murder with me, he was the most easygoing, affable man I'd ever met. Having him annoyed at me made me feel discombobulated.

Cal and I disagreed. That never bothered me because we'd actually started our relationship with him investigating me as a suspect. Oh, to hear him tell it, he never thought I murdered Banning, but I thought he thought I did, so we were definitely at odds, even if he didn't know it. I smiled over the thought, but that just made Dick scowl even harder.

"We had tea, for pete's sake," I said. "She loves trying to civilize me with her proper British tea."

"Nothing else?" he asked, his eyes narrowing, as if he could hone in on my expression and tell if I stretched the truth.

I sighed. I could lie and stay out of trouble, but I didn't lie well. "Tea. And I told Cathy about me being a grandma and told her I was staying out of the investigation..."

He just shook his head as if disappointed in me.

"Tea. Just a proper British cup of tea. Well, proper if you don't mind it was less than hot, but not quite cold."

He still looked annoyed.

"Maybe I can make it up to you," I tried. "We could go look around our set one more time, now that Duncan's releasing it."

"Well, I don't know," he said slowly.

"We could find something major. You know that's how it works. We stumble on something that seems small and later find out it was anything but. And we can talk about the *Mass*

Murder pilot. Mom'll come up with some wonderful way to kill the priest."

And so we walked back to *Cereal Killers*, bouncing ideas off each other for *Mass Murder* as if they were tennis balls.

"We're in Erie, Pennsylvania," I said.

"Erie?" he asked. He'd gone home with me a couple years ago, not so much to see Erie, but because he loved my mom.

Dad never minded their BFF relationship and seemed to genuinely like Dick as well. He'd been the one to offer to make him an honorary Mac.

My mom had seconded the idea wholeheartedly.

I took it as a further sign of our altered relationship. Until my Uncle Bill and then me, all Macs were physicians. Even my brothers' wives were doctors.

My parents were willingly adding a non-doc on purpose to the family now.

"You know I've wanted to set a show there and we have a lot of Catholic churches. Anyway, the story is set at St. Clare's of Erie, PA. I read somewhere that St. Clare of Assisi is the patron saint of screenwriters or maybe it was patron saint of television. Either way, I like it."

I shrugged. "We'll Google it, but let's run it for now. Father Murphy is the parish priest of St. Clare's. Three of his parishioners have died under suspicious circumstances. Oh, wait," I said.

"What?" Dick said.

"Father Murphy has his deadly illness, but no one knows it at first. All the dead parishioners had some disease. The cops suspect the priest of some kind of mercy killing. You know, I'm dying and I can save them the pain ..."

"Oh, yeah," Dick said. "And he dies."

"Yeah, absolutely dead. It looks like suicide, so everyone thinks he did the mercy killings and then took his own life. What no one knew was Father Murphy and Sister Mary Faith were best friends. She knows there's no way he'd kill someone or himself. But no one else believed her. She's old. I mean, really old. Uses a cane or a walker. Sister Mary Faith."

"I think nuns are named after saints and Faith, while churchy, isn't a saint." Sometimes Dick was like a dog with a bone. He found something and just kept growling over it.

"That's beside the point. She's tiny, frail and old, but has this huge, indomitable spirit. She's not going to let her friend, Father Murphy, be blamed for murders he didn't commit. And for taking his own life. Sister Mary Faith has a sidekick, a young novitiate, Gabby."

"Gabby?" Dick said laughing. I don't think that's very saint-sounding either.

"Fine it's a character description more than her name. Maybe Sister Mary Faith calls her that as a nickname. Gabby has long stream of consciousness monologues. Mary has a running gag of suggesting orders who live in silence to her."

"Do they still do that?" Dick asked.

"There's a Carmelite place in Erie. It's all walled and fenced off. I'm pretty sure they're silent. Anyway, Gabby and Sister Mary investigate the murders to save the reputation of the priest and vindicate his name."

I happily threw out ideas and Dick kept asking questions, making me rethink or clarify.

We didn't write anything down. This was Dick's forte. He'd take my Gabby-esque stream of consciousness prattle and turn it into an outline.

Then we'd both punch holes in it and refine it.

But I felt that now familiar rush of excitement over the idea. That moment when you know that you've got something solid with potential.

We poked around the prop room and found nothing. We looked in all the weird nooks and crannies and found nothing. We checked our offices and the writers' room and found nothing.

"If anything was here, it's not now," I said.

Dick nodded and agreed. "They'll figure it out."

"I hope so."

"And it looks as if we're gainfully employed again."

I smiled. "Have I mentioned lately how much I love working with you?"

"No, but let me just say, ditto."

CHAPTER NINE

"Now what?"

"I take you to bed and make love to you all night," Cal said.

I hadn't realized I'd said the words out loud, but obviously I had. I laughed. "Yes, there's that, but I was talking about the investigation."

He grimaced. "Ouch. We are definitely turning into an old, married couple."

"If I live to be ninety, my feelings for you will never get old," I assured him.

He kissed me then, just to seal my promise.

There was really no need. So many times throughout a day, I'd look at him and think, *this man*. Even with my vivid imagination, I couldn't think of a scenario where that feeling would diminish.

When we broke apart, he prompted, "The investigation?"

I nodded. "Now what do I do? After Dick and I finished, I put on my act for more than a half dozen people at the studio. It was a great act about not being involved with the investigation and being so very traumatized by the murderer's warnings. I didn't get anywhere."

"If you put out the word, then hopefully the notes will stop. And Quincy, Duncan *will* figure this out. He really is good. He's an intuitive detective. He sees patterns in chaos.

It just takes a while to collect enough information to find the pattern."

I thought about him staring at the set.

Maybe he'd already seen something that he didn't realize yet.

"You're right," I admitted. "I've done what I can. I'll hope it's enough and trust your baby detective. I want Hank to come home."

I hated not having Hank at home, but I didn't want him here until we were sure the threat was gone.

We'd FaceTimed after dinner and he was over the moon about his extended visit at Tiny's.

"And then, Sheila said…" He filled me in on his day. Afterward he informed that Uncle Sal cooks better than Aunt Tiny. "And Caesar and I decided to switch who gets the air mattress and the bed. I'm in the bed tonight. Aunt Tiny said she'll make us hot chocolate for breakfast."

He threw the last part in to see what I'd say. I was not a hot chocolate for breakfast kind of mom. At least not for the kids. For me personally? Hot chocolate went perfectly with my well-hidden cinnamon Poptarts.

I waggled my eyebrows to let him know I'd noticed the breakfast hot chocolate, but wasn't going to complain. "I miss you, sweetie, but have fun."

"Yeah, I will."

"Love you," I said, but the screen had gone blank. "I don't think staying with Caesar is traumatizing him," I said to Cal.

Cal pulled me into his arms, then led me to our room. And for a moment—well, to be accurate, much more than a moment—I forgot my worries.

But after Cal fell asleep, those worries crept back in.

I watched him sleep for a while. That first day, that first murder, when this hunky cop had walked over to me I'd had a brief fantasy that he wanted me. He did...to question me about the murder scene I'd accidentally cleaned.

Somewhere along the line, he wanted more than that.

Somewhere along the line, he'd become so much a part of me I wasn't sure I could function without him.

I got out of bed without waking him, and made a cup of hot chocolate—Hank had put it in my head and I knew the thought wasn't going anywhere until I'd had a cup—and then I took it to the dining room and I stared at my board.

I kept coming back to Tony Michna's picture.

He'd said that his dad cheated on his wife repeatedly.

Who was Brad Michna cheating with now?

Well, not now. But before he died. Who was he cheating with?

I looked at the clock. It was eleven.

That felt super late to me, but then I was about to be a grandmother. It wasn't late for my older boys, so I couldn't imagine that it was super young for a kid Tony's age.

I picked up the phone and dialed his number.

"Hello?" came a groggy voice on the other end of the line.

"Oh, Tony, I'm so sorry. I woke you," I said stupidly. "This is Quincy, we met at—"

"I remember," he said, sounding a bit more awake. "What can I do for you?"

I could lie and make up some excuse, but instead I said, "I was talking to the investigator today and was thinking about your dad. I just remembered something you said about him cheating..." I paused. "Sorry, that sounded harsh."

"No," Tony said with a huge sigh that I suspected had absolutely nothing to do with being woke up. "It sounded like the truth. He cheated on my mom and on Emmy, too."

"Do you know who his current girlfriend was? That might help the investigator."

"I did tell him that Dad cheated repeatedly. Dad said something about her working at the studio."

Bingo.

There it was. The connection between Michna, his family, and the studio. Baby cop hadn't told me but I didn't take offense. I knew from vast experience that cops didn't share what they knew, even when they wanted me to share everything I knew.

It wasn't fair, but I understood.

"Do you know her name?" I pressed.

"He called her Mitch, which was a weird nickname. That's the only reason I remember it. He had too many women over the years to keep track of otherwise."

"Did he say anything else about her?" I asked.

"Just that *Mitch* worked at the studio and she'd broken up with him because she found out he was married. He was pissed. Normally he didn't mention his girlfriends to me. I didn't approve of them and he knew it. But this Mitch pissed him off. He didn't like that she'd been the one who'd done the breaking up. We didn't talk much and it kind of hurt that rather than asking about me and my life, he railed against a woman he knew I didn't approve of. I hadn't remembered that about her nickname before," he said.

"Thanks, Tony. You already told the detective all of this?"

He paused. "Most of it, I think. She broke up with him, not the other way around," Tony said very seriously. "So I don't see a jilted lover motive."

I didn't want to mention that if the girlfriend worked at the studio, that was a connection to someone who had a personal relationship with Michna and where the body was found.

I sighed. "Yes, there's that. But still, maybe if the detective can find her, she'll know something more. And if you're not sure you told him all of this, you might want to call him tomorrow."

"Okay, I'll call him first thing," Tony said.

"Sorry I woke you up. This has all been playing over and over in my head."

"No problem—mine too. I've been a mess lately. Dad and I weren't close, so you'd think his not being here would hardly make a ripple in my life. But it does. I don't know what to do about it."

He'd said the same thing to me at the funeral.

And again, my heart ached for this young man. Every child should feel that they are the center of the parents' universe.

"Maybe that makes it hurt more," I said. "Thinking about what could have been … what should have been. But here's a bit of wisdom I picked up along the way, you can't control who your family is. You can't make them be what you want them to be. You have to accept them as is. But the family you're born in isn't the only family you're destined to have."

For years I'd felt like an outsider with my family. "I love the family I was born into and I adore my kids, but my family's so much broader than them. My writing partner is like a brother to me. My business partner is a sister. One of my ex-husband's ex-wives is like the daughter I never had, and my one son's wife is a daughter, too. My family is always evolving and growing and all of it is more than just a blood relationship. It's about love. Your dad cared about you in his own way and you mourn him. But you can go out and build a new family."

There was a long stretch of silence on the other end of the phone, then Tony finally said, "You're right."

"I tell my kids that I know everything. That might be a bit of a fib, but this, this I know." It had taken me a long time to realize it, but it was the truth.

"Thanks, Quincy," Tony said.

"If you start to feel lost, call me. I mean it." And I did. I didn't know this man well, but he reminded me of my boys and I felt very protective of him.

"I just might. And I will call the detective first thing tomorrow."

"Good night," I said.

"Night."

I hoped he got some sleep.

My hot chocolate was now chocolate milk, but I took a sip anyway. Talking about Peri made me realize I owed her a phone call. I missed her. When Jerome divorced me I thought my world had come to an end, but in retrospect his divorcing me had led me to … well where I was now.

And where I was now was a marvelous place.

The boys were grown and living worthwhile lives.

Eli was married and was going to make me a grandmother.

I had Cal and Hank, and friends and family.

I had a career I didn't plan on, but loved.

I just needed to put my latest dead body to rest and get back to enjoying this life I'd been blessed with.

I finished my chocolate milk and went back to bed. I snuggled next to Cal and he didn't wake up as he threw an arm over me and pulled me close.

And I couldn't help but thinking again, how lucky I was.

The next morning, Mom called at seven.

Yes, seven a.m.

As in seven in the morning.

Geesh.

After my late night, I woke up groggily as I picked up my cellphone.

I noticed that Cal was gone.

Darn. I'd wanted to tell him about "Mitch" first thing.

"Quincy, this is your mother," Mom announced, as if I hadn't seen her name and picture in my caller ID.

"Good morning, Mom," I croaked. "Is something wrong?"

"Oh, the time-change. Sorry. It's ten o'clock here and I was thinking about you. I wanted to check in and see what's going on with your zombie."

"I'm fine. The zombie's still dead—not normal zombie dead, but dead-dead—and Dick and I have a new idea…"

At some point I sat up as we chatted. I happened to catch a glimpse of myself in the chest of drawer's mirror.

Wow. My hair had taken the term bed-head to a whole new level of awful.

Whenever we'd done a morning scene on *Cereal Killers* I'd lobbied for a realistic approach, but I'd always been overruled.

Which is why the characters always woke up with reasonable hair. If it was disheveled, it was sexy disheveled.

I glanced at the mirror again.

I was definitely not sexy disheveled.

But I was going to win the issue on the new show.

Ten minutes later, I said, "Mom, I just woke up and have to pee. I'll talk to you soon."

"If you hear anything more, call," she said.

"I promise," I said.

"Love you."

The words seemed to come easier the older she got.

"Love you, too," I said.

After I'd taken care of nature's call and my hair—which was still a bit Medusa-ish, but better—I padded out to the kitchen, desperate for coffee.

Yet another reason I loved Cal...he'd made the coffee and it was still hot in the insulated carafe.

I'd barely taken a sip when Tiny called on the way to taking the boys to school and I chatted with her for a sec, then Hank.

"Can I stay another night?" Hank asked.

"I'll talk to Aunt Tiny," I said.

"How about I come over after I drop off the kids?" she asked over the car's speakerphone.

"Cal left me a full pot of coffee and I'll share," I offered, which I decided made me a very good friend.

"See you soon," she said then hung up.

I was on my second cup of coffee when she came in carrying briefcase and a small white bag.

"Donuts," she announced as she held the white bag aloft.

That was how I knew she was a true friend...she sensed my need for something before I was even aware of it myself.

I well and truly needed those donuts.

We ate donuts, drank coffee and talked about Mac'Cleaners.

"I talked to Theresa yesterday. She's still training Coreen, but says it's going well. We'll be opening that new office in Napa next month."

Tiny reached in her bag and pulled out a binder. We talked business with the ease of old friends. As the Mac'Cleaners discussion slowed, it morphed into baby news...

"We should be talking about a shower," Tiny said. And for a moment, I had a glimpse of my friend more than a decade ago right before her wedding to Sal.

"It takes time to plan something like this right," she said. "And of course your mom and sisters-in-law will want to come to down for it, so they'll need time to clear their schedule and book their tickets."

"Shower?" My horror at throwing a party must have shown, because she grinned.

She reached into her briefcase again and pulled out an even bigger binder. "We need to start planning. You know Peri will be here and—"

"We?" I said with relief, knowing by *we* she meant she would mainly take control of the shower.

Party planning was Tiny's joy as much as it was my terror.

"*We*," she said again for emphasis.

At some point I got lost in her maze of theme ideas.

"As long as it's not zombies, I don't care," I said.

She laughed. "LeeAnn does so much volunteering for environmental and animal groups, I thought we'd do a baby animal theme. Why don't you call her, double check the dates with her and ask for a guest list of people she'd like to invite. Then we'll get serious?"

I thought about asking if the last hour was her being less-than-serious, but didn't because truly, I didn't want to know the answer.

So on top of a zombie killer who was annoyed with me, pitching a new series to TPTB, and my son spending repeated nights at a friend's house, I had to worry about a shower…and all my family coming in town for it.

I spent the morning with Tiny, the afternoon with Dick and the evening…that was all just me and Cal.

No threatening zombies or notes.

Cal and I had agreed that if things stayed quiet, we'd pick up Hank on Sunday. Tiny kept reassuring me he was welcome as long as I needed him there.

Maybe the zombie killer threat was over.

It had been quiet.

Maybe I was in the clear.

The next day was Friday.

Just two more days until Hank came home and hopefully things settled down to a more normal rhythm.

Mom called again, but this time at a more respectable nine o'clock.

"Oh, a baby shower. I got your email and I know that if it's in Tiny's hands, it will be a huge success," my mother said as she drove to the office from the hospital.

I could tell she was on Erie's Peach Street because of her frequent grumbling about the traffic.

Yes, my mother complained to me about Erie's one always-busy street.

That's right.

One.

Oh, there was traffic on other Erie streets, but Peach Street was home to the city's mall and had become a shopping mecca. It was always busy.

Locals called it Peach Jam.

Cal, being an LA guy, laughed the first time he experienced Erie's *Peach Jam*.

I'll confess, I laughed with him because the "traffic" was... well, not.

"Oh, come on," my mother mumbled.

"Mom you called me," I reminded her.

"Yes. I called to say I talked to your sisters-in-law and we think we could all make it the weekend before Christmas. I talked to Tiny and she assured me she can pull everything together by then."

What on earth could go wrong with planning a shower the week before Christmas?... asked no one ever.

"...and," Mom said, letting me know the good news wasn't over yet. "Your Dad and I are going to come out for Thanksgiving. I talked to an agent and she'll have a list of homes for us to visit while we're there."

"Okay," I said, feeling overwhelmed.

So much for my optimistic hopes for a normal rhythm to my life.

"Are you sure it's okay?" my mom asked.

I heard a vulnerability in her voice that I rarely heard. After so many years of a rocky relationship, we both still occasionally felt as if we needed to tip toe around the other.

"Mom, that's wonderful," I said trying to infuse more enthusiasm into my voice. "Hank will be thrilled."

"Is anyone else coming in for Thanksgiving?" she asked, then said, "Turn already. What do you want, an invitation?"

I ignore her outburst and simply answered her question. "LeeAnn and Eli will be here. I don't think Miles or Hunter will. But everyone said they were coming home for Christmas."

"Oh, that's wonderful," Mom said. "I'll have my secretary looking for a house we can rent over Christmas."

"I—" started to protest.

I didn't have the room and we both knew it.

"Seriously, honey. We'll all come down and spend some time. You know what I always say about guests?"

"They're like fish ... both stink after a few days."

"Right," she said, then paused and asked, "And you talk to Cal. I want to be sure you're both on the same page about us coming to spend more time in LA."

"Mom, I don't have to talk to Cal or anyone else. We are all looking forward to you being here more often."

She swore again, then sighed. "I'm pulling in at the office. I'll get everything arranged here and contact you with our itinerary."

"Great, Mom. Have a good day. Love you."

"You, too."

I glanced at the clock and hurried out of the house. I'd promised to meet Dick at the studio.

My mind turned from dead-dead zombies to family and holidays and babies.

I sat in Beth's kitchen on our set waiting for him, fantasies of a new baby playing in my mind.

What would the grandkids call me? Grandma? Nana? MeMa? Busha?

Maybe we needed to work a grandma into the new show? She could be the novitiate's grandma and want to help. She'd be able to say things two nuns wouldn't.

And she'd knit.

I smiled as I looked around the set.

With everything else going on, I hadn't properly celebrated the fact we were going to get to spend more time with our *Cereal Killers* family.

The set felt like an extension of home.

Maggie's was sleek and contemporary, Joanne's was bohemian. But Beth's was slightly run down and filled with antiques. There was cast iron hanging on the walls. Beth's was my favorite.

Her cast iron pans reminded me of home. Griswold cast iron was made in Erie, PA. I had at least half a dozen pans at home. Some of it was over a century old and it still worked.

I liked that idea of function after a century.

It was odd to sit on a quiet set. Normally, there was the hustle and bustle of people moving about.

Now, it was so quiet.

Dick and I had a meeting with Joanne in an hour.

I heard footsteps and turned, "Dick, I—" I stopped mid sentence.

It wasn't Dick.

It was Cathy's dialogue coach ... well, not Cathy's. *Dead Man Walking's* dialogue coach.

Ann looked as startled as I felt. "Sorry. I didn't know anyone would be here."

I laughed. "I'm just waiting for Dick. We have a meeting."

"I heard rumors that you were going to do some *Cereal Killers* specials for HeartMark. You're going to start shooting again soon?"

I nodded feeling that happy excitement all over again. "Yes. We're thrilled about the movies."

"That's nice." She didn't look as if she thought the news was nice. She looked nervous.

Very nervous.

And maybe sick. Ann had dark circles under her eyes and her skin was waxen.

"Ann, is something wrong?" I asked.

"Wrong?" Her eyes darted from side to side and she looked everywhere but at me.

"Wrong," I said. "Did you come to see me about Steve or Cathy? Is there something wrong with them?"

My mind had no trouble coming up with a number of horrible reasons for Ann to come talk to me. Cathy was sick. Steve was sick. They were having marital issues ...

She shook her head. "No. I didn't think you'd be here. I didn't think anyone would be here."

I felt a flood of relief, followed by a small zing of awareness.

Maybe Cathy and Steve were okay, but something was wrong here.

I must have looked puzzled, because she said, "I needed a minute to think and, like I said, I thought your set would be empty."

"Ann?" I didn't know her much at all, but I hated seeing someone in such obvious pain.

I might not be a doctor like the rest of my family, but that much was part of my DNA.

"I haven't been sleeping," Ann admitted. "I thought it would get better, but it's getting worse. Everything's a mess and everywhere I turn, there you are."

"Pardon?" I asked, confused now.

She turned on me, anger rather than nervousness in her eyes. "You. Face it Quincy, you're a maid and a writer. You're not an amateur detective, you just write about them."

"I know that," I assured her.

"You act like you're *Perry Mason.*"

Now, that was a blast from the past. That was an older series than *Murder She wrote.* "That seems like it might be a series before your time."

Some of the anger seemed to fade as she said, "My grandmother loved it."

I nodded. "Listen, I know I'm not a detective. I tripped over"—on top of—"the body. I didn't set out to find myself in the middle of this."

"So walk away," she said.

"I've told everyone who would listen that I'm not investigating. I'm leaving it to the professionals. I can't stay away from the studio. I work here, Ann," I said gently. "I work on this stage. And you don't. So once again, what are you doing here?"

This time she wore a deer-in-the-headlight expression. "You know, don't you?"

I had no clue what we were talking about or why she was here, so I didn't say anything.

Ann looked exactly like my boys looked when they were in trouble. They didn't want to tell me, but they needed to confess. During those times, I'd discovered that not saying anything was so much more effective than guessing.

"Listen, it was an accident," she said. "I didn't mean to…"

Oh, my goodness…

She did it.

I had no clue why or how, but Ann Abner DeMarco killed Brad Michna.

Ann Abner.

Ann Arbor.

Michigan.

Mitch.

I sat still as a church mouse. If she'd killed once, she might kill again and I didn't want to do anything to remind her of that fact.

If I were writing this on *Cereal Killers*, my character would casually reach into her pocket and dial someone on her cell. She'd let them listen to the entire confession.

Or she'd know how to make her cellphone record the confession.

I wasn't nearly that slick.

If I reached in my pocket, Ann might think I was reaching for a weapon and shoot me. If Michna was any indication, she was a good shot.

I was not about to get shot today.

I had a lifetime still with Cal. I had all four boys. Hank was still so little and needed me. I had friends. I had a job I loved and a business I loved.

And I was going to be a grandmother.

No way was I missing that.

"I didn't mean to," Ann said.

Frankly, I'm sure most killers said something like that. At least they did on my show.

I just waited quietly. Not really in hopes of finding out more but because I didn't want to be her next victim.

"We'd dated, you see," she said.

I didn't mention I'd already figured out she was Mitch.

"I didn't know he was married until we were well into the relationship. When I found out, I broke things off. But Brad was not someone who liked to have a woman dictate to him. He said we'd be done when he said we were done. He called me and showed up at my house at random times for months. You don't know how scary it was to come home and find he'd been in the house. He'd leave dirty dishes in the sink, or the television on. Sometimes he left notes. Those were the worst."

She looked at me guiltily and I knew she'd left the note at my house.

And she'd been at the Halloween party. She could have tucked the other note in my pocket.

I finally ventured to say something. "What happened?"

She still stood center stage, just beyond Joanne's kitchen. "I thought it was over. I thought he was done, but then I came to work and there he was, being zombified. Brad had been an extra on dozens of shows. Eventually, I put it together and realized he was the host of the *Behind the Scenes* podcasts. I knew what him being on my show meant. He was going to do a podcast on *Dead Man Walking*. He was going to try to dig up something ugly. I knew a few people who had secrets they wouldn't want shared. People who were cheating—though I'd never be able to judge them because I'd inadvertently cheated. People with a drug problem. People who..." She looked at me helplessly. "You know how it is. Fans don't seem to realize that the actors are just people. Most of them are actors because they have problems."

"When you have problems it's sometimes easier to be someone else," I said quietly.

She nodded. "That's it. I didn't want Brad making things worse for them. I didn't want them to be embarrassed or hurt. They're my friends."

"So...?"

"So, I brought him here. The show had gone late. I brought him over to your stage because I didn't want anyone to overhear us. I wasn't planning to come in. I mean, I figured the door would be locked. But Brad had a key and let himself in. He seemed to know his way around."

"He did a piece on us," I said, "and was an extra for us. He must have got a hold of a key and copied it."

"Yeah." She nodded. "He led me to the writers' room for our talk. I should have just left, but I followed him. I was so angry I forgot to be afraid of him. I told him to leave or I was going to tell Cathy and Steve. He laughed, then hit me hard across the cheek. My ears were ringing afterward. He told me I wasn't going to say anything to anyone. If I did, he'd tell them..."

She stopped and looked at me helplessly.

I'd been afraid, but suddenly I knew I didn't need to be. Whatever happened, I didn't think Ann had set out to kill Michna. I patted the stool next to me. She came over and sat down.

"You can tell me," I said. "I'll figure out how to help you."

"Cathy's always spoken highly of you and I can see why." She sat quietly for a moment, as if trying to gather her courage to finish the story.

"I told him I would tell Cathy and he laughed and said he'd tell her about my affair with Steve. Brad had been so crazy jealous when we were dating. He'd accused me of having affairs with other men more than once. But I hadn't. I wouldn't. And Steve?" She shook her head. "He's wonderful, but definitely not my type. I said as much and Brad said he'd seen us go on our date."

"You and Steve?"

She nodded. "It wasn't really a date, though we joked and called it that. He had tickets to the opera and Cathy hated it. She told him I'd said I'd like to learn more and he took me. If he weren't a writer, he'd be a teacher. He was so patient as he explained the story and…" She started to cry now. "It was a lovely night. We were just friends. And Cathy knew. I said that, and Brad laughed again and promised when he was done telling her the story, she'd believe him."

She was sobbing harder now.

"My head hurt, my ears were still ringing and I reached up my hand, as if I were going to hit him back. He blocked my hand and hit me again, harder this time. My head hit the table from the force. When I righted myself, he was standing there with a gun pointed at me. He called me horrible names and said he was sure I'd been cheating on him the whole time we were dating. I said I wasn't the one who was married."

If Brad Michna weren't already dead, I'd be tempted to do him bodily damage for hitting, hurting, and humiliating this girl. I took her hand in mine.

"He sat the gun down on the table and reached out and grabbed my…" She shuddered. "He was so crude and said since I was putting out for Steve, maybe we should get together for old times sake.

"I picked up the gun and pointed it at him. I said that right now, made up like a zombie, his outsides were as ugly as his insides. I wouldn't let him touch me again. If he took another step…"

She broke down again.

I patted her as she sobbed. When she'd cried herself out a bit, I asked, "What happened then?"

I felt the shudder as it moved through her body. "He laughed and said it was a prop gun. I don't know why I pulled the trigger. I believed him. I believed it was a prop gun and still, I pulled it and I hit him. I think he looked stunned, or maybe he died instantly and I just imagined he looked surprised. He fell and I just left. I don't know why I didn't call 911 or security. He'd hit me twice. He'd threatened me with the gun. I went home and threw up the rest of the night. I kept trying to figure out what to do, but it was like thinking through mud. My head hurt and my vision wasn't right. To be honest, I can't believe I drove home. I know better, but I wasn't thinking clearly. And… well, the next day Cathy called me about the body on your set. And said the cops were all over the place. We weren't going to shoot that day because it was a zombie. I wasn't an actor or an extra and she didn't think they'd need to talk to me, but if they did, she'd call. I told her I was sick. We'd had a flu sweeping through the show."

"So what did you do next?"

"I went next door to Mrs. Eddy's house and begged some acetaminophen off her, then went back to bed. It took a couple days to feel close to myself, and by then it was too late. I called in sick at work for a couple weeks. Every day I'd wake up and say it was the day I was going to call the cops. And every day I was too afraid to come forward."

I remembered that first body. I'd been terrified of going to prison for a crime I'd only cleaned. I'd had nightmares about being tattooed like my uncle. I understood her fear.

"I told myself if they arrested someone else, I'd say something, but I hoped they'd never figure out anything. You seemed to be everywhere, and I left the notes hoping you'd steer clear."

"But I didn't," I said.

"No, you didn't."

"Do you still have the gun?" I asked, praying she didn't have it on her. I was relatively sure I was safe, but not a hundred percent.

She nodded. "Yes. I hid it. I wanted to have it as evidence that it was me in case someone else got accused." She looked up at me, her eyes still puffy and teary. "I wouldn't have let that happen," she said again.

"You have to come forward," I said softly.

Her shoulders sagged. "I know that."

"But I have a friend who's a lawyer. Let's call him first. If you turn yourself in, it will look better. I don't know what will happen. But he'll help."

"Why? Why would you help me? I wrote those terrible notes to you and left a body for you to trip over."

"Because men like that—men who take advantage of women..." I shook my head. "It was self-defense."

"I'm not sure that's how the cops will see it," she said.

At that moment, Dick stepped into sight. "I have it on good authority that's exactly how the cops will see it."

I raised an eyebrow and Dick mouthed the word, *baby cop*.

Duncan had been here with Dick. He'd heard Ann's confession.

Dick jerked his head toward where Duncan had been, but he'd left.

I couldn't figure out why for a minute, then I realized Duncan had left so Ann could turn herself in.

I quirked my eyebrows at Dick, asking for confirmation. He nodded. "I think you should call Sal and get Ann over to the police station as soon as possible."

Duncan had left so Ann could come in on her own.

"I'm afraid," Ann said.

"Don't worry. It will be all right," I told her.

CHAPTER TEN

S olving Michna's murder seemed anticlimactic.
Not that there's anything wrong with that.
Personally, I preferred it.
Sal took Ann to the police station.
Duncan was waiting.
He'd heard the confession and was sympathetic.

The next few weeks were busy, and though Ann was charged with involuntary manslaughter, Sal felt certain she'd get a plea deal, since both Duncan and the DA were sympathetic.

It also helped that Ann's neighbor, Mrs. Eddy saw the bruises when Ann had come over and asked for acetaminophen. Mrs. Eddy also gave a statement about how confused Ann had seemed. She said she'd tried to get Ann to let her take her to the emergency room and spent the next few days checking on her frequently.

The media had a great with headlines like, *LA's Favorite Maid Does It Again*. And *Quincy Mac… Cleaning Up Hollywood One Murder at a Time*.

It was awful.

The good news was having my name back in the headlines pushed HeartMark into speeding up not only our *Cereal Killers Movie* of the week, but also our new series, *Mass Murder*. It was going to be a busy new year.

But first I had to make it through the holidays.

And the baby shower.

"Quincy," Tiny said, nodding at my glass.

My ice cube had melted and my "baby" was floating in my lemonade.

"My water broke," I screamed, more excited than was seemly. But if I had to suffer through planning a party, I wanted to win at something, even if it was only a shower game.

I know that Tiny and Peri did most of the planning with Honey helping with food. They love parties. But I'll confess, of all the parties I'd ever been involved with, my grandchild's shower had to be one of the best.

Peri had found the game. You froze plastic party babies (I still hadn't decided why such things existed) in ice cubes and the first person's who melted and yelled, "My water broke," won.

"I don't want the prize, but I just wanted to note that I won," I assured the crowd with a grin.

Within moments, LeeAnn's sister's water broke and she won the beverage carbonation thing.

I don't know how Peri managed it, but the games were actually fun. My favorite wasn't really a game. It was decorating disposable diapers with sayings. I used a red marker and wrote, *Whatever this diaper looks like, remember Grandma says Daddy's were worse.*

I made myself laugh over that one because it was true.

Comedy's first rule was, real life is always the funniest thing.

All the men came back for the last hour of the party.

Cal found my side. "How bad was it?" he asked as we looked at Big G's crowded restaurant.

"Not bad at all. We're going to be grandparents. I'm not sure how that happened, but Cal, it's going to be amazing."

He kissed my cheek. "It is."

I looked out at the crowd. Everyone I loved was here. My parents, my brothers and sisters-in-laws, my friends...

I had everything.

Even if my career turned to dust, I'd still have everything.

"Is it time for the reveal cake?" Tiny asked.

"Yes."

I held Cal's hand as LeeAnn and Eli cut into the cake to reveal a pink meringue in the middle.

"A girl?" I said.

I didn't know anything about girls, other than having been one.

I'd just assumed it was going to be a boy.

But a girl?

"Are you okay?" Cal asked.

I burst into tears.

Not pretty actress tears, but happy, ugly tears that led to my nose running.

No, not pretty at all, but heartfelt.

"We're going to have a granddaughter," I said.

Cal hugged me to him and at some point I found my way to hugging LeeAnn, then Eli, then...well, I'm pretty sure I hugged everyone at the party. And for a person who wasn't prone to hugging, that's a lot of hugs.

But my joy knew no bounds.

I was going to be a grandmother and have a granddaughter.

The happy thought kept bouncing through my mind.

"I got you a piece of cake," Cal said, suddenly at my side again. He handed me a plate. A plate with a big piece of cake...with no bottom frosting. You know, that pretty little rib of frosting they run where the cake and plate meet?

"You ate my frosting," I said.

He looked extremely guilty as he shook his head and smacked his lips.

"Frosting thief," I accused, then I laughed and forgave him. He had brought me a corner piece after all, and everyone knew that corner pieces were the premium cake pieces.

Yes, I forgave him, but I wasn't going to forget.

Revenge would be mine.

But for the day, I simply reveled in the happy gathering of my family. Christmas was just a few days away and...

I was going to be a grandmother of a girl.

EPILOGUE

I was working on a *Mass Murder* script when I got the call. I wove through traffic like I was Keanu Reeves driving a bus through the city traffic that made my mother's *Peach Jam* look like a country lane.

I got to the hospital in record time and went through a security check before I could enter.

Some might have found it annoying.

I found it comforting that my granddaughter was safe here.

I knocked on room 317. When Eli called, "Come in," I threw open the door and there she was.

My son was holding my granddaughter.

"Mom, meet Beatrice Quincy."

They'd named her after me. I couldn't help myself...I started to cry.

I held the tiny baby with dark curly hair and intense blue eyes that seemed to lock with mine. We were going to be close.

I managed to look long enough to make sure LeeAnn was okay, then I went back to admiring our newest member of the family.

I tried not to overstay my welcome, but it was hard handing baby Bea back.

"Here's your little Bumble Bea," I said, laughing.

As I drove at a much slower pace back towards home, I passed by a tattoo parlor.

I remembered all those years ago worrying that Cal was going to throw me in jail and I'd have to get a tattoo like my uncle.

Oh, I knew worrying about a tattoo was easier than worrying about going to jail.

I'd worried about it … a lot.

Without realizing I'd made a decision until I'd made a decision, I went into the parlor, signed a bunch of papers, and showed my ID.

Then pulled up an imagine on my phone.

I took off my sock and pointed to the inside of my heel, just below the ankle.

I felt pretty sure it was an area that wouldn't wrinkle or sag … two of my biggest fears about my prison tattoo.

The image was small.

Miniscule even.

But when I finished, I left with a tiny bumblebee on my heel.

I'd never again have to worry about prison tattoos.

I left to go home to my home to my husband, Hank … and the life I adored.

December 2017

Dear Reader,

The title of this book means a lot to me. I thought about going with something more zombie oriented, but I knew this title was the. You see, my mother loved Quincy. After I wrote the first book, *Steamed*, she drew up a list of other potential cleaning titles. This was her favorite. I have the list taped to the side of my roll top desk. And when I started the book, I knew this would be the title. Mom passed away in July and as I worked on Quincy's fifth story, I'd occasionally come across something I knew she'd laugh at. More than once I reached for the phone to call her ... and realized I couldn't. I think that made Quincy's evolving relationship with her mother even more poignant for me. Quincy and her mom have grown closer over the last few years and it was important to me to make sure her mother came to town in this story.

As for her mom mentioning taking pottery classes, well if you follow me on social media, you know that I went back to school and I've been taking pottery classes. I'll confess, my glee runneth over. I try to contain it, especially as I'm in an eight a.m. class with a bunch of bleary-eyed college students. I said something about masking my glee in class one day, and one of the other students assured me I was an utter failure at it. My glee leaked out all over the place. I'm sure Quincy's mom is enjoying her class as much as I've enjoyed mine! A special thank you to Professor Hubert. I'm pretty sure my constant questions might be a bit much, but he's always sweet about taking time to explain a concept or skill. He's been especially helpful as I mull a new cozy mystery series. There might be a ceramic connection ... stay tuned.

Finally, I want to thank all of Quincy's fans. I've had a few characters who get their own fan mail. Pearly Gates, Nana Vancy and Quincy Mac are the most popular by far. Thank you everyone who has followed her from that first accidental cleaning of a murder scene to this, her dead-dead zombie story I thought I'd put her to bed in the fourth book, but here she is again. So even though I think this is the last book, I'm not saying never. Really, thank you!

Holly

PS. If you have a moment, please leave a review for Polished Off on your favorite online book site.

PPS. Now that you've read my Maid in LA Mysteries, try *Can't Find NoBODY.* I'm including an excerpt for you.

Can't Find NoBODY
copyright Holly Jacobs

SPLAT!

When Markie Walkowicz and her friends used to whack each other with snowballs during rare Philadelphia snowfalls, that's what it sounded like.

Splat, splat. They'd scream at the top of their lungs as snowballs whizzed back and forth.

It wasn't the fact that it was cold enough for snowballs that brought the word *splat* to Markie's mind on this particular Monday morning. It was the fact that the porch was rushing toward her face at an alarming rate.

Or rather, *she* was rushing toward the porch as she'd tripped and fallen.

Splat!

She landed hard in an inelegant heap. It took her a stunned moment to suck some frigid air into her rather deflated lungs.

It figured, she thought.

It just figured.

Markie was always more accident-prone when she was running late. And she was running so late this morning that she quickly decided a fast fall on the porch was better than the myriad of other accidents she might have attracted. Last time she was running this late, her front tire was flat.

She examined her throbbing knee, noting she had a hole in her stocking. She was going to have to go back in and change them, which meant she was going to be even later, but probably not as late as when she'd had to change that tire.

Panty hose might be torturous to put on, but they weren't nearly as difficult to manage as lug nuts.

Markie got up and immediately spotted what she'd tripped over.

It was a man.

A decidedly blue-looking man, laid out in front of her door.

A blue man wearing a green and orange plaid suit that was decades out of style.

"Mister?" she said, even though she instinctively knew she'd get no response.

The man's arm was thrown over his face. She reached out to touch his hand.

It was cold.

Markie screamed as she scrambled to her feet.

Screamed like a girl.

Loud, long and piercing.

Marquette Ann Walkowicz was the type of woman who prided herself on avoiding such feminine clichés as shrieking. She just didn't do it. Not about bugs, or even snakes.

No, Markie Walkowicz was not the type of woman who screamed like a girl.

But tripping over a dead body on the porch on a Monday morning when she was already late … well, that warranted a scream or two.

She stood for a moment, staring at the ugly plaid suit the dead man was wearing. It was so hideous that it was easy to focus on.

What to do?

What to do?

It was like trying to think through mud. Her brain had shut down as she stared at row after row of ugly pumpkin-orange and avocado-green plaid.

What to do?

It wasn't as if she had personal experience with discovering corpses on a front porch.

What to do?

She read a lot of women's magazines and they always had helpful hints on everything from hairstyles to how to please a man in bed, but she'd never seen an article about what to do when you trip over a dead body.

What to do?

What to do?

911.

Those three little numbers popped into her mind, glowing like some sanity-saving beacon.

She'd call 911 and they'd know what to do.

Markie did a ginger little leap over the body and into the house and then slammed the door.

Not only did she slam the door, she locked it, throwing the dead bolt and hooking up the chain.

After all, who knew how the man had died?

Maybe there was a murderer lurking in the bushes.

She rushed to close the front drapes and then ran to the phone. Her fingers were shaking as she punched those three numbers.

"911," the operator said. "What is the nature of your emergency?"

It took a second for her scream-strained vocal cords to respond to her command that they now produce a normal sound.

"There's a dead body on my porch," she finally managed in one quick burst.

"Your name?" the operator asked, no hint of shock or panic.

"Markie Walkowicz."

"And your address is?" the woman asked, continuing her calm questioning as if people called her all the time because they'd found bodies on their porches.

Markie had worked at a vast number of jobs over the years, but she was sure she'd never want a job where getting calls about corpses on the porch was par for the course.

"Ma'am, your address?" the operator asked again.

Markie told her.

"I've dispatched a unit," said Miss Calm-Cool-and-Collected. "Now, we'd better check the man—"

"*We'd?*" Markie interrupted, with a hint of a girl-scream back in her voice.

"—and feel for a pulse," the woman continued.

Purposefully, she forced herself to beat back her rising panic and speak in a usual tone. "You said *we* and by *we*, you mean me. You want *me* to go feel for a pulse. Sorry, ma'am, I'm not touching him again. There is no pulse. He's blue. And before you ask, there is no way I'm putting my lips on his for mouth-to-mouth. He's blue and cold. I don't need a medical degree to know that no amount of CPR is bringing him back."

There was a blue man in an orange and green plaid suit on her front porch.

As the realization sank in, Markie began to shiver uncontrollably.

There could be a murderer out there right now as well, peeking in the windows and watching her, deciding how he was going to kill her.

Feeling exposed, Markie took the phone and stepped into the coat closet.

She felt safer in its dark depths. Safer and just a bit warmer. The shivering slowed a bit.

"Did you recognize the man?" the operator asked, obviously having decided that she wasn't going to talk Markie into revisiting the body for either pulse-taking or CPR.

"I don't know. His hair was gray, so he was old. But his arm was sort of thrown up over his face so I didn't get a good look at him, and I wasn't moving his arm to get a better one. As a matter of fact, I don't know that I could move it. He felt sort of solid when I tripped over him."

"You tripped over him?" There was slight surprise in Miss Monotone's voice—the first hint of emotion she'd shown.

Markie had plenty emotion to spare, not that she could quite identify any one in particular. Her feelings were a mixed-up jangle at best.

"Yes, I tripped over him," Markie said. "He was right in front of my door, and it's Monday."

"Monday?"

"I was running late, and it's Monday, so I was in a hurry because I didn't want to spend the rest of the week trying to catch up. I have a meeting at the bank today, so I'm wearing business clothes instead of my normal jeans. I haven't even had a cup of coffee."

The fact that she was dealing with a corpse before coffee just seemed to make the situation worse. "Anyway, I was hurrying out and there he was … so I fell right over him and put a hole in my nylons."

"I see," Miss Armchair-Psychiatrist said.

I see. That's all she said, but Markie could hear a sort of a soothing quality in her voice, as if she were trying to calm a lunatic.

"I'm not crazy," Markie said.

"I didn't say you were. You're just upset about finding a body. I understand."

"I doubt that you do, unless of course you tripped over a dead body and found yourself next to a blue guy in an ugly plaid suit."

Obviously the operator couldn't argue with her logic, because she didn't even try. Instead she said, "Ma'am, there should be an officer there. Can you see him?"

"I shut the front door, but even if I hadn't, I'm in the closet, so no, I can't see anyone."

She had to give the lady credit—not only did she treat calls about dead bodies with professional detachment, but the operator didn't even comment about the fact that Markie was now in the closet.

She just said, "Well, you can get out of the closet and open the door now. The officer's waiting on the porch."

"You're sure?" Markie asked, thinking of murderers in the bushes.

"Positive."

"Okay. Thanks."

She hung up the phone and climbed out of the closet. Her muscles felt overstretched, as if she'd been doing aerobics all day instead of squatting on the closet floor. She walked stiffly to the front door.

"Who's there?" she asked, just to be on the safe side.

"Police, ma'am."

She opened the door.

A tall, blond officer stood there. He had a baby face and didn't look nearly old enough to be a cop.

Heck, he barely looked old enough to shave.

It was hard to trust a cop whom you might have been babysitting only a few years back. Everything about him was shiny and crisp, as if he hadn't had a chance to break in his uniform yet.

Her day just kept getting worse. A baby officer had ridden to her rescue. The murderer would probably make mincemeat of him.

"Do you want to come in?" she asked, figuring she could lock both herself and her kiddie cop safely away in the house, away from the murderer.

"I'm Officer Manning. You called 911 about a body on the front porch?" he asked, ignoring her question.

Markie looked down and felt a spurt of relief. The officer might be young, but he was good at being a cop. He'd removed the body so that she didn't have to deal with it again.

He was considerate. His mother was probably so proud.

"Yes, I'm the one who called," Markie said. "Thanks for getting rid of it so quickly. I don't think I could stand looking at it again."

"I didn't get rid of it," the officer said. "When I arrived, there was no body here."

"There was a few minutes ago," she blurted out, staring at the spot under the officer's foot where the body had been.

The officer looked skeptical.

"I tell you, he was here. A dead man in a plaid suit, laid out in front of my door."

"You're sure he was dead? Maybe he was just a drunk who decided to sleep it off on your porch," the officer suggested.

It wasn't just what he said that set Markie's teeth on edge, but the look he gave her. A condescending, why-me-first-thing-on-a-Monday-morning sort of look.

"Listen, I know the difference between *dead* and *drunk.* This guy was *dead.*"

"Yeah? How many dead guys have you seen before this?" he challenged.

That stopped her.

Other than her grandmother Ida, who had passed away two years ago, Markie had never even been to a funeral home before. "None really, at least not like this, but—"

"Markie?" came a voice she recognized immediately. A voice that came from a man she didn't want to see…

Check out <u>Can't Find NoBODY</u>.

Award-winning author Holly Jacobs has almost three million books in print worldwide. The first novel in her Everything But... series, *Everything But a Groom*, was named one of 2008's Best Romances by Booklist, and her books have been honored with many other accolades. She lives in Erie, Pennsylvania, with her husband and four children and two dogs, Ethel Merman and Ella Fitzgerald. You can visit her at http://www.HollyJacobs.com.

Other Holly Jacobs Books for Your Kindle

Romance and Romantic Comedy Single Titles

Briar Hill Road
Just One Thing
Same Time Next Summer
Not Precisely Pregnant
Can't Find NoBODY
Hung Up On You
I Waxed My Legs for This?
Her Second-Chance Family

Words of the Heart series
Book 1 Carry Her Heart
Book 2 These Three Words
Book 3 Hold Her Heart

PTA Moms Trilogy
Book 1 Once Upon a Thanksgiving
Books 2 Once Upon a Christmas
Book 3 Once Upon a Valentine's

Cupid Falls series
Book 1 Christmas in Cupid Falls
Book 2 A Simple Heart: A Cupid Falls Novella

Dear Fairy Godmother ... series
Book 1 Mad About Max

Book 2 Magic for Joy
Book 3 Miracles for Nick
Book 4 Fairly Human

Everything But... series
Book 1 Everything But a Groom
Book 2 Everything But a Bride
Book 3 Everything But a Wedding
Book 4 Everything But a Christmas Eve
Book 5 Everything But a Mother
Book 6 Everything But a Dog

Maid in L.A. Mystery series
Book 1 Steamed
Book 2 Dusted
Book 3 Spruced Up
Book 4 Swept Up

Perry Square series (A Holly Jacobs Classic)
Book 1 Do You Hear What I Hear?
Book 2 A Day Late and a Bride Short
Book 3 Dad Today, Groom Tomorrow
Book 4 Be My Baby
Book 5 Once Upon a Princess
Book 6 Once Upon a Prince
Book 7 Once Upon a King
Book 8 Here With Me

WLVH Series:
Book 1 Pickup Lines
Book 2 Lovehandles
Book 2 Night Calls
Book 3 Laugh Lines

Whedon Series
Book 1 <u>Unexpected Gifts</u>
Book 2 <u>A One-of-a-Kind Family</u>
Book 3 <u>Homecoming Day</u>
Book 4 <u>A Father's Name</u>

Valley Ridge Series
Book 1 <u>You Are Invited</u>. . .
Book 2 <u>April Showers</u>
Book 3 <u>A Walk Down the Aisle</u>
Book 4 <u>A Valley Ridge Christmas</u>

Short Stories and Novellas

<u>Able to Love Again</u>

<u>The Book</u>
<u>Labor Day</u>
<u>There He Was</u>
<u>13 Weeks</u>
<u>Bosom Buddies</u>
<u>Cinderella Wore Tennis Shoes</u>

Nothing But… Short Story Series:
Book 1 <u>Nothing But Love</u>
Book 2 <u>Nothing But Heart</u>
Book 3 <u>Nothing But Luck</u>

Love all the books? Try a bundle or boxset!
<u>Short Stories for the Overworked and Under-Read Anthology</u>
<u>Maid in L.A. Mysteries Bundle</u>